MU01025772

Checked Out

The Village Library Mysteries, Volume 1

Elizabeth Spann Craig

Published by Elizabeth Spann Craig, 2019.

This is a work of fiction. Similarities to real people, places, or events are entirely coincidental.

CHECKED OUT

First edition. April 2, 2019.

Copyright © 2019 Elizabeth Spann Craig.

ISBN: 978-1946227430

Written by Elizabeth Spann Craig.

Thanks to all the librarians who made me feel at home
in different libraries throughout my life.

Chapter One

I'd just finished checking out some cookbooks for a young mom when the library doors flew open and two sopping wet boys rushed up to the circulation desk. I stood up immediately because of the state the boys were in.

"What's wrong?" I asked.

The older boy was so winded that he just gasped out something completely incoherent, so the younger one said, "There's a cat out there! He's in a culvert. He could drown!"

Another librarian said quickly, "You go. I'll cover the desk."

I hurried out, jogging to keep up with the two boys as they shoved open the door and scrambled out into the pouring rain. It was coming down in sheets and had been for the last couple of hours. I was immediately soaked through and shivered even though I could feel the humidity coming off the pavement in waves.

"Where is it?" I asked urgently. Surely a cat wouldn't be able to hang on in a drainage ditch culvert for very long with the amount of water that must be gushing through it. There was a crack of thunder overhead and I winced.

"Over here! When our mom dropped us off, we heard a cat crying," yelled the older boy who seemed to be getting his breath back.

The culvert was in a low-lying area on one side of the parking lot and water was gushing down into it to drain off. The last thing I needed was for the boys to get swept in. "Thanks, guys. What are your names?"

They told me and I thanked them again. "Go inside now and use the library phone to call your mom and tell her to come bring you some dry clothes."

"No way!" said the boys in chorus.

The older one, who had a stubborn set to his chin, added, "We'll stand back. But we want to see what happens."

I gingerly knelt down to peer into the concrete, open-ended culvert. Sure enough, caught on some brush inside the pipe, was an orange cat. He stared back at me with intelligent green eyes and let out a pitiful cry.

I leaned forward, now getting the knees of my black slacks soaked as I reached out for the cat. "Come here, sweetie," I crooned.

The orange cat's eyes shifted to the right, and he gave another cry but didn't move toward me.

"Come on, baby. You're safe. Just come with me." I crawled carefully ahead into the large culvert, feeling the water surge against me and keeping my hand on the side of the pipe. Then I stopped, squinting as I peered ahead. There was a second cat in there, slightly farther back and still in the brush as the water continued flowing faster and faster.

"Can one of you boys get some help from inside the library? There's another cat in here," I called out. "And get one of the librarians to bring a flashlight from the storage room."

From what I could tell from inside the culvert, they both took off, sounding like a small herd of elephants as they sprinted toward the building.

I kept crooning to the orange cat. "Is that why you won't come out? Your friend is in there? You're such a good friend, baby."

The cat gave another sad cry, and I felt my heart pound in my chest. I shivered again and reached out to the cats. Neither one moved.

I heard the kids running back outside again and adult voices with them this time. I turned to see Wilson, the library director, hurrying toward me, clutching a flashlight and also, inexplicably, a rake, which he held aloft. He was always distinguished-looking with prematurely white hair, rimless glasses, and an omnipresent suit. A rather stylish elderly lady, an occasional patron of ours, trotted right behind him, holding an open umbrella and grasping another.

"What's with the rake?" I asked.

He said, "The kids said the cats were stuck on some brush. The custodian thought we could rake the brush forward." He handed me the rake.

"Ah. Good point. Although I'm a little worried the rake will scare them farther into the pipe. I'm going to have a hard-enough time reaching them as it is."

He pulled something out of his rain jacket and shoved it at me. "Here. Also from the custodian."

I propped the rake against my leg as I took a pair of leather work gloves from him. "Perfect! Remind me to kiss him."

The patron said importantly, "And I'll try to keep you all dry."

Far too late for that, but I appreciated her efforts. At least the boys, apparently not wanting to get even wetter than they were, huddled under the open umbrella with her. "Hurry," the older one implored me.

Wilson and I peered into the culvert again and the sad little orange face looked mournfully back at me. The cat turned his head to look at the other cat again and then turned back to me, giving me a hopeless look.

"Okay," I said briskly, faking the confidence I didn't feel. "Here's the plan. I'm going to try to get the cat that's farther back out first. I suspect the orange cat won't come out without her. But since they're so far back, I'll use the rake to pull the brush toward me a little first."

"Slowly," clucked the patron, forgetting about the rain and stepping outside the spread of the umbrella before hurriedly ducking back underneath it as she was pelted with drops.

"Yes," I said under my breath. Nothing to it. Just another day in the life of a librarian in Whitby, North Carolina.

I reached down and smiled what I hoped was a reassuring smile for the cats before feeling completely ridiculous. Would cats even recognize facial expressions? Instead I said, "Good babies. Just hold on."

The orange cat took me at my word and did indeed hold on, grimly. The other cat, still only partly visible, wailed in distress as I ever so slowly crept as far into the culvert as I could and then even more slowly extended the rake to one side of the brush. Finally, after what seemed like hours, I was able to hook the rake behind the pile of leafy branches, pine straw, muck, and sticks and gently pull the mass toward me. Then I did the same on the other side of the mass of brush, managing to get the whole mess a couple of feet closer to me.

Still, I needed to get closer, so I abandoned my crouch and went fully on my stomach. The patron clucked again. "Do be careful! That water is scary!"

"I could hold on to your feet," said Wilson reluctantly. He glanced down at his impeccable suit as if resigning himself to getting it immersed in the drain water. "I really don't need one of my librarians floating away in the storm drainage system." He pressed his lips shut. I'd worked for different directors, but never one quite as uptight as Wilson.

"I think I'll be okay," I said quickly, envisioning falling flat on my face in the process, especially since I wasn't the most coordinated of people at the best of times. At this point, it seemed good to calm down Wilson just as much as the poor cats. "But if you could grab me if I start floating away? I don't think the pile of brush would stop my progress."

He stooped down on the edge of the culvert, grimly poised to rush in and seize my legs if needed. And, to make things worse, the rain came down even harder.

I crept to the cats, crooning under my breath. I gave the orange cat a light, reassuring rub, and he purred at me, although he remained steadfastly on his branch. I turned my attention to the other cat, reaching out a tentative hand. The cat's eyes were huge, and I was worried she was hurt and might lash out in a panic.

Gently, I took off a glove to tickle her under her fuzzy chin and she half-closed her eyes in relief. I replaced the glove and continued sliding forward through the gushing water.

When I could scoot up enough, I put both my hands under her arms. She gave a loud cry that made me freeze and made the kids and the patron cry out, too.

"We have a hurt cat," I said. "Can one of you call a veterinarian?"

"I will," said the lady, her voice anxious.

I carefully cradled the cat in my arms and started the awkward process back . . . this time sitting completely down on the floor of the culvert and scooting forward inches at a time with the water up almost to my chest. I turned to look at the orange cat, who was now looking much more relaxed and cheerful. He gave me a little chirping meow and I couldn't help but smile. Whoever he was, he was a charmer.

When I made it out of the pipe, the boys and the lady cheered. Wilson simply looked very relieved at not having to file a disability claim. "The vet is on the way," the lady said.

"Wilson, can I very gently hand this cat over to you and get the other one? She can go in the breakroom," I said. "I think her leg is injured, so I'll try to be careful."

Wilson reached out his arms and I slowly transferred her to him as the cat breathed heavily.

The lady said, "Do you have any old towels or anything to make her comfy until the vet gets here? And to dry the poor thing off?"

Wilson smiled through bared teeth as the tabby clawed his shoulder in alarm as he shifted her. "I'll see what I can find in the custodial closet."

He set off to the library, and I edged my way into the culvert again. The orange cat was very alert and seemed to want to help me as the rain continued gushing into the pipe. "You can do it, baby," I whispered to him. As I held out my arms to him, he pounced into them and snuggled his wet, furry head against my neck. "Hey sweetie," I crooned. Then I carefully crawled back out to more cheers.

The patron said, "I'll see if he found the towels. Otherwise, I can run to the dollar store for hand towels." And she trotted off, absently taking the umbrella with her.

It didn't really matter because the boys and I were soaked to the bone already and so was the orange cat. We couldn't possibly have gotten any wetter than we already were. The boys reached out to rub the cat, and he purred loudly.

We hurried back inside and found our progress had been tracked by what seemed like everyone in the library. They'd all peered out the many windows of the building and cheered for us when we came in. "Give a round of applause for our two heroes today: Noah and Mason!"

The library applauded and cheered and the boys, delighted, gave mock bows.

One of the patrons came up to me. "I captured the rescue on video on my phone! I'll tag the library in it and post it online."

I grinned at her. "That would be awesome." Nothing like an adorable couple of cats in an action-packed video to bring traffic to the library social media sites.

Wilson dug up what appeared to be some ancient beach towels and had done his best to pat dry the injured tabby cat. He handed me a towel and started briskly rubbing dry the orange cat as he purred his appreciation.

Another patron quietly watched our progress from the door. "I could run out and get some cat food and a litter box," he said.

"It wouldn't hurt," I said, turning to smile at him. "The vet is on the way, but I'm not sure how long the cats will need to be here in the meantime. Even if both of them need to go to the vet tonight, we could use some food and litter for now."

Wilson raised his eyebrows at me as the patron hurried away to run the errand. "All right, Ann. What's our end goal here?"

I leaned forward to gently tickle the tabby under her chin. The last thing I wanted to do was spook Wilson. But honestly? The Whitby Library would be an amazing place for a library cat. Instead I said, "What do you think? I haven't really had a chance to think this all through. I was just concerned about getting the cats out of the culvert."

Wilson looked at me over his glasses as he finished rubbing the orange cat dry. "We should focus on finding them good homes."

"You wouldn't happen to need a friendly cat, would you?" I asked lightly as the orange cat rolled over on his back and purred.

Wilson didn't seem to notice that I was joking. He frowned at me and impatiently pushed his glasses up his nose. "I definitely don't need a cat, no." Then he said, "But *you* probably do, don't you, Ann? Living by yourself?"

I snorted. "If I wanted to *see* the cat at all, I'd have to keep it here. You know I'm here practically daily and on weekends. A cat would be sorely neglected at my house."

Wilson sighed. "All right. So here's the game plan. We'll let the vet have the cats. We'll take the cats back here after the vet is done and post pictures to try to find them homes."

I reached out and stroked the orange cat. "Perfect. And I'll try to screen the patrons who display interest, since I know most of them pretty well."

Wilson stood up, brushing the cat fur off his suit slacks and looking relieved. "That's settled, then. Hopefully, we can find money in the budget to pay the vet."

One of the other librarians opened the lounge door and introduced the vet, who was carrying two cat carriers. Wilson and I quickly introduced ourselves and I gestured to the tabby and said, "That's the one who seems injured."

The vet gently examined her and nodded. "Her leg is broken, for sure. I'm going to need to take her back to the office and set it." She knelt by the orange cat and rubbed and talked to him as she examined him next. "This guy looks to be in perfect shape, however. He's young and strong. In fact, if I had to guess, I'd say the injured cat is probably his mother."

I felt myself choking up and blinked impatiently a few times. There was something about animals that always got to me. "He wouldn't leave her. I didn't even see the tabby at first and the orange cat was determined to stay put until we helped her."

The vet straightened up and said, "He sounds like a really special cat. I'm going to take him with me, too. I'll want to check both cats for microchips and give them their shots. And fix them, of course, too, if they haven't been spayed and neutered."

Wilson winced a little as if wondering what the bill for all of the vet care might be.

"That's perfect. Thanks so much." I paused. "The two cats seem really close to each other. Is it all right to separate them?"

The vet said, "I think that may just be the circumstances in which they found themselves. Usually kittens are separated from their mom at about ten to twelve weeks old. The orange cat is far older . . . likely one year old. If it makes you nervous, you could always suggest a reunion later and see how it goes. And also monitor how the cats behave when they're apart from each other."

"Good ideas," I said. "Thanks. I don't want to create any problems for these sweeties."

The vet smiled at me. "That's no problem at all. And no charge for any of this—I'm just grateful you went beyond the call of duty and were able to rescue these cats."

Now Wilson was beaming with relief at the vet, which made me smile, myself.

"All in a day's work for a librarian," I quipped. And I wasn't stretching the truth. You never did know what was going to happen at the library. Except most of the time the adventures revolved around a jammed copy machine and a botched storytime.

"I'll bring the orange cat back here tomorrow," said the vet as she carefully put the cats into the crates. "Possibly the tabby, too. I'll have to see how she does."

"So soon?" I asked, wrinkling my brows. It seemed like major surgery to me, but then I hear of people getting pacemakers in outpatient, so what do I know?

"He'll be fine and will even have slept off the anesthesia by then. The tabby might be well, too. They'll just need to stay quiet. I have a feeling that won't be a problem here," she added with a twinkle in her eye.

Wilson snorted. "When was the last time you were in a library?" he asked. "This place is a zoo most days. Even without a couple of cats."

The vet frowned. "Would you prefer if I kept them at the office and tried to find an owner for them there? Or perhaps just brought the orange cat back here? Would that make things easier?"

Wilson said, "Why don't you bring the tabby back here as a *temporary* measure? Perhaps we can try finding out if these cats have an owner. Worst case scenario, I'll see if one of our patrons might be able to give her a good home."

"Sounds good," said the vet. "And, again, I'll waive the charges for their care."

Wilson put a hand up to his forehead as if it had started aching.

"I'll take a couple of pictures of the cats and post them on the bulletin boards here to see if anyone knows who they might belong to," I said.

Wilson made a face. "Perhaps that would have been better when they were snuggled into the beach towels and not crouched in carriers."

"I'll just open the crate doors and use my flash," I said. I snapped a picture with my phone and then looked at the results. "Ugh." I tried again. "All right, this one is a bit better. Regardless, if the pictures don't find her a good home, then she can stay here at the library while she heals up and I'm sure someone will want her."

Wilson carried one of the carriers and the vet the other and they trundled off to the parking lot while I picked up the towels and put them in a trash bag to take home with me to wash later. Then I printed out flyers with the cats' pictures and 'found' on them and posted them several places in the library. After that, since my feet were still sloshing in my shoes, I retreated again to the breakroom.

Wilson came back in a few moments and quietly regarded me as I took off my shoes and dabbed fruitlessly at them with paper towels.

"I think you're forgetting something," he said.

Those words made me catch my breath. If there was one thing I hated, it was being late for something. "What is it?" I asked. "Don't tell me we have some sort of bedtime storytime tonight for the kids."

"You have that blind date tonight," Wilson said with a chuckle. "You asked to leave here early, remember? Don't you want to slip out of here and head home to change clothes?"

"Noooo. Ugh, I'd totally forgotten." One thing about being single in your early thirties was that there were gobs of well-meaning patrons dying to set you up with someone. It was both touching and incredibly frustrating. "I have an extra outfit here in case of emergency," I answered automatically.

Wilson said, "I know how organized you are and I don't doubt it. But, and forgive me for bringing it up, your hair and makeup leave something to be desired. It's doubtful they're appropriate for a date. It's even debatable whether they're appropriate for working in a library."

I craned to see myself in the mirror over the breakroom sink. Wilson was absolutely right. My shoulder-length black hair was stuck to my head, and the ends were still dripping tiny rivulets of rainwater down my soaked black blouse and khaki pants. My mascara and eyeliner had run, giving me raccoon eyes. There was also the fact I had muddy paw prints and cat fur all over me.

I grinned at Wilson. "Actually, this is perfect. Now I can scare him off and not have a second date."

Wilson snorted and shook his head at me. "You're being silly, Ann. For all you know, this guy could end up being someone you could have a real relationship with."

"It's a *blind date*. Nothing good ever comes out of a blind date. Believe me, I know. I could likely write a book on them I've had so many. It's been pouring all day and all I want to do is get home and get in my pjs and cuddle in my bed with a book. Besides, I'm not really in the mood to give a relationship a go right now. Things are busy at the library," I said.

Wilson said, "Things are *always* busy at the library. If you're waiting for that to change, you're going to be single a long time. And you're in your early 30s now. I've known you to go on dates, but never second dates. Not that it's a bad thing being picky, of course. It's just sometimes it feels as if you're burying yourself in the library instead of venturing out to find someone to spend your life with."

I quirked an eyebrow at him. "You're starting to sound like some of our elderly female patrons. Or the guys in the library film club."

He ignored this. "Besides, that patron was being sweet to set you up on a date, wasn't she?"

I sighed. "Emily is always sweet. She can't help it. But I have the feeling she's thinking more of her great-nephew than she is me. This evening has disaster written all over it. But you're right—maybe I'm subconsciously trying to sabotage it."

"As your director, I'm urging you to go home and get ready." He paused and then continued in a rare show of kindness, "We have plenty of help here today. We'll manage just fine. And tomorrow, we have our new children's librarian coming in, so we'll have even *more* help," said Wilson.

I smiled at him. "Got it. Okay, I'll go ahead and head on back. I'm taking the wet beach towels with me to wash. And you're right—tomorrow will be fantastic with a new librarian here."

"Of course, you've done well filling in for the various storytimes," he said stiffly. I hid a smile. I didn't quite believe him.

"Thanks. But somehow, I don't think working with children is exactly my gift," I said. I was definitely enthusiastic about the children's lit. I loved everything from *Babar, the Elephant* to *Don't Let the Pigeon Drive the Bus*. But somehow, the kids always seemed especially squirmy when I was in charge of storytime . . . which I had been for several months while Wilson struggled to fill the children's librarian position.

I lugged the trash bag of wet beach towels to my aging Sub-aru and drove home. Fortunately, home was only a few minutes away, not that anything was very far away in Whitby. It's a beau-tiful mountain village with lots of old buildings and even older trees. It's the kind of place families vacation in to escape the city and to see fall leaves change on the Blue Ridge Parkway. There was also a quiet lake nearby, perfect for fishing and lazy after-noons on the water.

My house was admittedly more of a cottage, although I loved the place. After my mother died when I was little, my great-aunt took me in and raised me there. When she passed away five years ago, she left the cottage to me. The outside was a riot of rose bushes, gardenias, and azaleas. Flowering vines ran up the stone exterior and the entire effect was one of something out of a storybook. Which, as a librarian, suited me perfectly.

For the most part, I loved my neighborhood. It was a street of older homes, but the kinds of older homes with lots of char-acter. A couple of them were old Craftsman houses, which I thought was really cool. Everyone tried to keep up with their yards, with varying degrees of success.

I was lucky in that my aunt had planted an amazing garden and I was only tasked with keeping it up. What's more, every time I saw the garden, I thought of her. It used to be the mem-ories gave me a sharp pang in my chest from missing her quick wit, but now they finally made me smile . . . it had taken a while.

Most weeks I can spend some time maintaining the yard, even if I didn't really know at first what I was doing. I did a lot better with it after I'd checked out a few books and magazines from the library—and even better when I'd invited our county extension office to give a talk about caring for local shrubs and flowers. I still had plans to plant a vegetable garden in the back-yard someday like my aunt had done yearly. After an honest assessment of the amount of free time I had, though, I reluctantly shelved this idea for later.

There were only two people on my street who made me uncomfortable, and in different ways. One of them was Zelda Smith, an older woman with henna-colored red hair who chain-smoked constantly.

The other person on my street who could easily throw me for a loop was a guy who'd just moved in down the street. He seemed cheerful, witty, and handsome and somehow turned me into jelly when he glanced my way. As yet, I hadn't even spoken to him, but I'd seen him interact with other neighbors.

It looked like my challenge today was going to be Zelda. I was getting my mail at the end of my driveway and she suddenly materialized from the other side of a bush.

"There you are!" she said with her gravelly voice. I jumped.

"Ms. Smith!" I said in an accusatory voice. "You scared the living daylights out of me."

"Sorry," she said, although the glint in her eyes told me she was anything but. "I have a really tough time catching you at home."

"That's because I'm rarely here," I said, trying to keep my tone light. "Usually, I'm at the library. I've mentioned this before. You're more than welcome to find me at work if you need to."

Zelda made a face. "I don't read."

I said politely, "There are many other reasons to come to the library. We have great study areas. And you can also check out music or stream movies from our website. Or even take a class. We have some interesting options coming up. I'd be happy to sit down with you and show you all the different ways you can use the library. There are some fantastic services."

I could never seem to help myself from being an evangelist for the library. I could tell, though, my propaganda was not having the desired result. In fact, Zelda now appeared even less inclined to visit.

"I'm all right, but thanks," she said in a completely disinterested voice. "What I really wanted to talk to you about was the homeowner association."

Apparently, Zelda's entire mission in life was to pressure me to be on the neighborhood homeowner association board.

This, however, was not in line with my own plans. If I didn't even have time to plant a vegetable garden, I certainly didn't have time to serve on our homeowner board. Plus, I'd had several neighbors complain to me about the board and their intrusive policies.

Everyone was fine with many of their rules: rolling the trash and recycling bins back after collection and not allowing the yards to get too out of hand. But they also ruled on homeowner construction . . . whether they were allowed to put up a deck or a porch or even a backyard treehouse. That seemed to rile up my neighbors and was another reason why I didn't want to have a spot on the board.

"I think we've already discussed it, Ms. Smith. I appreciate all the work the board does, but it deserves to have a member who has the time to do a really excellent job. I simply don't have that kind of time. I'm frequently working both at night and on the weekends. And I don't take on anything unless I know I'll do a great job."

Zelda Smith narrowed her eyes. "It's your turn, Ann. Your late aunt, God bless her soul, was a legend on the board. Such a gift she had! I know she would want you to take a turn."

The mention of my aunt was something of a low blow. "I don't think she'd have wanted me to lose all of my meager free time, Ms. Smith. I wish I could talk longer about this, but I'm afraid I need to go." I hesitated. As a librarian, my single focus was always helping people. It was very, *very* hard for someone to ask for help with something and me not provide it. I said slowly, "There's a new neighbor on our street. I don't know his name, but maybe he'd be interested in being on the board."

"That young man?" Zelda's expression indicated what she thought of youth in general. It also showed she didn't really consider me as being part of that group, although I was pretty sure he and I were about the same age. "Someone told me he was a radio DJ." She spat out the words as if music was potentially poisonous.

"I don't know him," I added quickly. "I only thought perhaps he was worth contacting." I pulled out my key and headed to my front door with determination. "See you soon, Ms. Smith."

I unlocked the front door and pushed it open with a relieved sigh, turning on a few lights as I came in. The cheerful interior never ceased to make me smile with its overstuffed gingham chairs and sofa, the multicolored scatter rugs, and the book-lined walls.

I opted for a quick shower, mostly to feel warm again finally after being out in the rain and drain water for so long. I put on a pair of black slacks and a gray three-quarter sleeve top. I pulled my black hair back into a loose ponytail, put in some small silver hoop earrings, and put on the gold locket I always wore. It looked like I was about to head back to work, but I wanted to wear something conservative for this date my patron had set me up on. I wasn't planning on being encouraging, despite Wilson's reminders to keep an open mind. At least there was one good thing; the rain had finally stopped.

I couldn't help but sigh as I climbed back into my car. It would have been so nice to stay at home, pull on loose-fitting yoga clothes, warm up some leftovers from last night, and finish reading *The Alchemist*, which somehow, I'd never gotten around to reading. Then I told myself to get a grip. It was one date and it would make Emily very happy. Besides, my date was probably just as reluctant as I was. Maybe it would be something he and I would even laugh over. I tried to remember his name. Roger. Roger Walton. I said it under my breath a couple of times to make sure it set in my brain.

One thing I thought was odd was that he'd invited me over to his house for supper. In my long and disaster-ridden dating experience, I'd definitely learned one thing: meeting for coffee or lunch was safest. It was quick enough that you didn't feel trapped, but long enough to give you some sort of impression of the person you were with. This made me wonder if Roger hadn't been part of the dating scene for very long. Maybe he was recently divorced or had just ended a long-term relationship. His great-aunt Emily definitely hadn't provided many clues.

I pulled up in front of a large house with a manicured yard. It looked like one of those lots where they put a huge house on top of two small lots. The sun was trying to peek out from the clouds, and I could see purples and pinks of an approaching sunset over the mountain peaks. I got out of the car, smoothing down my clothes and the wayward hairs from my ponytail. I sighed as I walked down the front walk. Emily had meant well, and it was really sweet that she'd wanted to set the two of us up. But I could never figure out why everyone was so determined to force single people into pairs. Taking a deep breath, I rang the doorbell, a few butterflies in my stomach. And waited.

After a minute had passed, I hesitantly rang the bell again. I didn't want to sound frantic to get in and start this date, but it was the appointed time we'd agreed on. Wasn't it? I frowned and checked my phone to re-read the text thread in case I'd lost my mind. But there it was . . . six o'clock. At his house.

Maybe the doorbell wasn't working. I rapped at the door a minute or two later, shifting uncomfortably on my feet and starting to feel foolish standing at his door for so long.

Then I sniffed the air. Did I smell charcoal? Maybe Roger was planning a cookout and had neglected to tell me simply to walk around to the backyard. At any rate, he definitely wasn't answering the door, so I decided to try the backyard.

When I circled around to the back, squelching through the muddy lawn, I saw a barbeque grill smoking . . . and the body of my date on the ground beside it, a skewer through his neck.

Chapter Two

For a second, I stared at him, frozen. Then I rushed forward to make sure Roger wasn't still breathing and needed help. Finding no pulse and seeing that his eyes were open and unfocused, I took a deep breath, found my phone with shaking hands, and called the police as I carefully made my way back to the front yard again.

What must have been two minutes later, I could already hear a distant siren. And then another. And then another. In a town like Whitby, emergency personnel didn't have as much to do on a regular basis—and then all showed up in concert for a big event like this.

Another couple of minutes later, a police car, an ambulance, and a fire truck pulled up in front of the house, sirens wailing and lights flashing. And seconds after they arrived, every neighbor on the street was standing in their front yard, anxiously staring at the commotion. If I'd had any illusions that my blind date was going to be kept under wraps, they were now completely shattered.

I pointed to the side of the house as the policeman jogged toward me. "Around the back," I said, deciding not to tell him there was no need to run. I shivered and then felt my legs go a little wobbly. One of the medics noticed. "Sit down," he said firmly as he disappeared around the corner of the house.

I did as I was told. The tension of the blind date coupled with the shock of the discovery made me a lot more unsteady than I'd have thought. Working with the public as I did, I'd definitely had my experience in dealing with people who were ill and I'd considered myself someone who wasn't easy to faze. Apparently, though, this did not extend to finding dates murdered.

I sat on the curb as the first responders did their work in the back. I saw their pace slow as they realized it wasn't an emergency. The tone of their voices was grim.

A minute later, one of the medics came back to check on me.

"I'm fine," I said, feeling embarrassed. "I was just woozy for a second or two."

The medic left me to return to the backyard. The firemen left a few minutes later, and I waited for the policeman to speak to me. He was the chief, as I recalled. I tried to remember what I knew about him, including his name. He'd only been on the job for the last month and had moved here from another state, according to a story I'd read in the paper. He was a big middle-aged man, tall and solid with a steady gaze and a receding hairline.

I remembered when he'd moved in, he'd hosted 'coffee with a cop' as an opportunity to meet members of the community and to find out their thoughts on the town and safety issues. I'd thought it was a smart move, considering small towns can be insular and it can be tough to meet people as something of an outsider.

A few minutes later, he reappeared, looking serious. Spotting me still sitting on the curb, he came over and plopped heavily down next to me.

"You okay?" he asked, peering at me with concern.

"Yes. Sorry, I was just a little unsteady for a moment and one of the medics told me to take a seat. I can follow you somewhere else if you need me to?" I asked.

He started to shake his head and then glanced down the street at the neighbors still staring at us.

"Small towns," I said with a little laugh.

He nodded and said, "Maybe it wouldn't be such a bad idea to sit elsewhere. It's kind of distracting having an audience. Do you think they'd freak out too much if you were to sit in the police cruiser?"

I shook my head. "Not as long as you didn't put handcuffs on me and shove me in the back seat."

He chuckled. "Don't think there's any danger of that, at least not right now. Murderers don't usually call their crimes in. Although I'll be sure to keep my eye on you."

We settled into the cruiser and he turned on the car to let the air conditioning run. He was definitely running too hot, with the exertion of running to the backyard and the stress of what he'd found. He cranked up the A/C all the way.

"First off," he said, sticking out his hand, "I'm Burton Edison, your new police chief. I don't think we've met before."

I clasped his hand. "Ann Beckett. I'm a librarian."

He nodded and continued, "Good to meet you, Ann. Could you tell me what happened? And your connection with the victim?" He glanced at his notebook. "One of the firemen identified him as Roger Walton. Is that correct?"

I nodded. "That's right. At least, I assume that's correct. I wish I could give you more information. I've never even met Roger. I arrived about five or six minutes before calling you. I was at work all afternoon before going home to change. A neighbor of mine, Zelda Smith and I spoke for a few minutes there," I said hurriedly. If I needed an alibi, at least Zelda could prove herself useful. "Roger was my blind date—we were set up by his great aunt, who is one of my patrons at the library. Roger didn't respond when I knocked and rang the bell, so I walked around the side of the house."

Burton grunted. "You probably could smell the grill, couldn't you?"

He was definitely sharp. I nodded at him. "That's right. I wasn't sure what he'd planned for tonight, but when I smelled charcoal burning, I went around the side of the house, figuring he just couldn't hear me. That's when I found him." I tried to keep my voice steady.

Burton jotted down some more notes in his notebook. "That's got to be the worst blind date on record," he said, glancing up to wince in sympathy.

I gave a dry laugh. "It is, although I've had a couple that rivaled it. My dating life has not been a particularly rewarding one."

A car pulled up behind us and parked along the curb. A blonde woman in her twenties hopped out of the car, eyes narrowed with concern at the sight of the ambulance and the police car Burton and I were sitting in. She strode up to us.

Burton unfolded himself from the car and stepped out. "Something I can help you with, ma'am?" he asked politely.

"Yes," she said in a rough voice. "You can tell me what's going on here. Why are there police cars and ambulances?"

Burton tilted his head to one side and then extended his hand. "I'm Burton Edison, the new Whitby police chief. I'm sorry, I don't think we've met."

"I'm Heather Walton," the young woman answered, impatiently pushing a strand of blonde hair out of her eyes. "My brother lives here."

Burton took a deep breath. I stood up and got out of the police car. "Here," I said. "I shouldn't be hogging the seat." In fact, I just wanted to get out of there, especially as a family member was being informed of a tragedy.

Burton seemed to sense I was edging myself away. "If you could stick around nearby, Ann, that would be great. I may need to speak with you some more."

"Back to my brother?" asked Heather impatiently.

Burton said, "Would you happen to have a picture of your brother? Of Roger?"

Heather sighed and whipped out her phone, flipping through the gallery before showing the police chief a photo. He nodded slowly.

"I'm very sorry to have to tell you this, but Roger is dead. He's been stabbed," said Burton, enunciating the words carefully as if to be as clear as possible.

Heather gasped, covering her mouth with one hand.

I walked away a bit, careful not to walk *too* far away since Burton had made a point about wanting to speak with me again.

Burton spoke with Heather for a while as the sun started setting. Before long, other cars pulled up, and I found the state police, the SBI, had arrived. I guessed Whitby was too small to have any sort of forensic department or to be outfitted with what they needed for a murder investigation. The SBI asked me the same questions Burton had.

While I was in between questioning, Heather walked up to me and gave me a tight smile. "I have the terrible feeling that I should know you, but I just can't place you. Were you dating Roger?"

Clearly, Roger hadn't confided in his sister, but then there probably were plenty of brothers who wouldn't. I said, "I'm so sorry about your brother. We weren't dating, but we did have a first date scheduled for tonight. That's why I was here. I'm Ann Beckett—I've seen you at the library. That's where I work."

Heather nodded. "Thanks. It's terrible realizing you recognize someone but not knowing from where. Of course, I know you from the library. I see you there every single week."

"Well, when you're used to seeing someone *only* at a particular place and then they're not there, it can be tough to place them," I said. I hesitated and then said, "Again, I'm so sorry about your brother. This must be a terrible shock for you."

Tears welled up in Heather's eyes and she impatiently rubbed them away. "Sorry. Roger and I were close and I just can't seem to wrap my head around the fact that he's gone."

"Were you coming by for a visit?" I asked sympathetically. If so, it was better that I found Roger than having his sister discover his body.

She hesitated. "More like driving past. I've been running errands this evening, just trying to get caught up. I've been at the pharmacy and gassed up the car and was on my way to the grocery store. When I saw the emergency vehicles, I just wanted to find out what was going on."

I said, "That must have been really scary to see it and to realize it was at your brother's house."

Heather nodded and then rubbed impatiently at her eyes. "Not as scary as what happened to you! The chief told me what happened. So, you walked around the side of the house to see why he wasn't answering the door and then you . . . found him."

I nodded and tried for a matter-of-fact voice, even though I felt a telltale tremor trying to work its way in. "That's right. And although I didn't know Roger, I'm sorry I didn't have a chance to even meet him. He sounds like he was a great brother."

A cloud passed across her eyes and Heather turned away for a second to look at the house.

I said, "I'm so sorry. It all just seems crazy."

Heather said slowly, "It does seem crazy. I can't believe it's happened. Whitby isn't the kind of town where murders happen. It wasn't even a random break-in. The chief said that, after a brief inspection, it didn't look as if anything was out of place in the house. There weren't any drawers pulled out or papers on the floor or any signs someone had been in a rush to search the house."

"Would they be able to tell from that? I'd think that a man, living on his own, might have a few drawers pulled out or cabinets open or whatever," I said. "That a single man might be a little sloppy."

Heather shook her head. "Maybe most men, but not my brother. He kept everything neat as a pin. He always cleaned up after himself. I don't think I've ever been over there and even seen as much as a coffee cup in the sink. But you're right—the police can't *really* tell until I go in his house and have a look. That might be later or might be tomorrow because he said they have to treat the house like a crime scene right now." Her voice trailed off at the words and a sad expression crossed her face.

"That's awful. I'm so sorry you have to go through that," I said.

"It's awful, but I want to help them find out who did it. After all, if it's not a robbery gone wrong, it sounds like it must be someone he knows. Someone with a grudge. And there's only one person I can think of off the top of my head who might have one. A woman named Mary Hughes."

"Is she a neighbor of his? Someone like that?" Maybe neighbors were just on my brain because they were all still out in their yards, gaping at us. I wouldn't be surprised if they started pulling out yard chairs and eating popcorn.

"No, Mary was a former coworker of Roger's," said Heather.

"You know, I never even knew what Roger did for a living," I said. "That was one of the things we would have been talking about this evening."

"He was an investment adviser. Not maybe the most fascinating of jobs to discuss on a first date," said Heather with a short laugh. "He'd been in that field since he got out of college. He counseled people on their stocks and bonds and helped people plan for retirement and stuff. Anyway, he and Mary didn't get along somehow. Roger had told me she'd been passed over for a promotion a few weeks ago—he'd received it, instead."

I said, "Well, that's just the way things go at an office, after all. Not everyone can get a promotion or you'd have an office full of managers."

"That's true. But from what I heard, she took it very personally. Mary thought she was more qualified to get the promotion than Roger was and she was really vocal about it. She made things very uncomfortable for Roger at the office every day," said Heather.

I could only imagine. It would be awful having to go into work and see someone who was bitterly angry at you all the time.

Heather added, "Then Mary was suddenly let go. You know how offices are. Anyway, she somehow acted like she thought Roger was at fault for that, too. According to Roger, anyway."

"You should make sure to let the police know," I said carefully.

Heather stared at me. "You don't think Mary could have killed Roger, do you? Just for being upset about something that happened at work?"

"I have no idea. I don't know Mary. But I think it sounds like something the police would like to know about," I said. "Where is Mary working now?"

Heather made a face. "That's part of the problem. She's apparently having trouble getting back on her feet again. She has a job at the tanning salon. I mean, I don't know Mary, but I've seen her walk in there when I drive by. Of course, there's nothing *wrong* with working there, but after she'd had this very professional job, it just seemed like it wasn't the best choice for her. Plus the fact that she never usually *has* a tan. The last time I saw her at the grocery store a few weeks ago, she was as pale as usual—as pale as me," she said with a snort. She paused. "Roger told me she'd been drinking a lot, too. It was almost like what happened to Mary at the office started her down this slippery slope."

We were quiet for a few minutes before Heather said in a more cheerful tone, "I do need to get back over to the library. I always have a book to read and in the past few months I *haven't*, and it's been the weirdest feeling. And now maybe I need something to distract me from—all this."

I nodded. "I'm like you. I have a weird feeling when I don't have a book I'm reading. Ordinarily, I'm trying to read two books at once so I don't usually have that problem."

Heather made a face. "I'd be totally confused if I tried to do that. I'd mix up the characters between the books or something."

"I'd probably do the same thing if the books were really similar. It only works this well because I pick two totally different books. One will be a novel and one will be a biography, for instance. What kinds of books do you like to read?" I asked.

"Oh, I'll read anything I've heard is good, but I especially like reading murder mysteries," said Heather. She winced and gave a short laugh. "Maybe I need to try something different, since I seem to be caught up in a murder mystery in real life."

I said, "You could. Although I do know a really fun murder mystery that should still manage to be an escape. Try *The Magpie Murders* by Anthony Horowitz."

She smiled at me. "Thanks for that. I'll run by the library soon."

A few minutes later, Burton pulled me aside to ask me a few more questions with the particulars of my movements before arriving at Roger's house, how long I'd waited at the door, and what I'd noticed when I'd walked around the back.

Before I left, he added, "And you said you work at the library."

I nodded. "I'm there most days. I'm actually not supposed to be working as many hours as I am, but I love it there."

Burton said slowly, "The thing is, I'm obviously very new in town. I'm guessing you aren't."

"I've been in Whitby most of my life," I answered.

Burton said, "How about if I bounced some ideas off you sometimes? Nothing official," he said in a rush, "but I'd like to get your perspective on the town and its residents from time to time. You're probably acquainted with a lot of folks with your job at the library. You have the kind of info that could be valuable for me. I don't want to tread on any toes with a big case like this—and my first really high-visibility one here in town."

I smiled at him. "That sounds like a great idea. I appreciate how sensitive you are about being new here."

"Well, I just don't want to go trampling in. I know small towns can be a little mistrustful of newcomers."

"How about your deputy? Does he know many people in town?" I asked.

He rolled his eyes. "Let's just say he's pretty antisocial. He keeps to himself. As a matter of fact, I might know more people in town than he does."

I suddenly remembered something. "Actually, you could help me out with something. I know you won't have a lot of time while you're working on this case, but I recently held a survey to see what programs adults might be interested in at the library. One of the most-requested things was a self-defense class."

Burton raised his eyebrows at this. "In Whitby? I wouldn't have thought there was a lot of need for that here."

My smile was a little more strained this time. "Actually, it was a suggestion I threw out there, so maybe the survey results were a little less than scientific."

Burton gave me an appraising look. "You're worried about your own safety? I get that you work in a public place, but so far Whitby has seemed pretty quiet."

I took a deep breath. "It's probably a result of my backstory. I was raised by my great-aunt here in Whitby because I lost my mother when I was eight. We lived in Charlotte then. It was really early to realize the world wasn't that safe of a place after all." I shivered, still remembering the months of nightmares I'd had after my mother's death and the kindness of my aunt when they happened.

Burton nodded slowly. "I'm so sorry. Of course, that's going to affect the way you see the world. And I'd be happy to give the class. Actually, it would be a good way for me to meet some more residents, so the sooner the better."

"I'll get it set up," I said. We might not have a lot of time to get the word out, but if I scheduled some posts on social media, we could still get a good group.

Chapter Three

I made it back home in a fog. I found something in the fridge to warm up and ate it without focusing on what I was eating. All I could think about was what had happened. I picked up my book and then put it down again and rubbed my hands over my face. Things were bad if I couldn't use my favorite pastime to escape. What I suddenly realized I needed was something totally mindless. Well, what I actually *really* probably needed was to go to sleep, but I sure didn't see that happening until I was able to unwind a little bit.

I picked up the remote and turned on the television. It hadn't been on for a while and, as a matter of fact, looked like it needed dusting. I settled on some sort of reality show that pulled me immediately in and settled down to watch the TV equivalent of cotton candy—decidedly un-nutritious but captivating as the rain started up again and poured down on the roof.

THE NEXT MORNING, I moved really slowly as I got ready. I'd had crazy dreams all night about cats and bodies and police and woke up not feeling at all rested. I took special care over my makeup, figuring some well-applied makeup could cover up most of the evidence of the rough night.

I used my key to unlock the library and turned on the lights. The old building felt like home. It was an old Carnegie library and a beautiful one. It was constructed in the Greek revival style and looked like an ancient temple. The bricks were a buff color and there was a low parapet around the roof with repeating embellishments in the cornice. The center of the roof was raised and boasted ornamental lions. The inside was cheerful and cozy with a fireplace in a reading area and comfy armchairs. It felt safe. Plus, naturally, the whole place smelled of books.

It wasn't long before Wilson came in, again wearing a rather solemn-looking suit. He said briskly, "How did your date go?"

I winced. "I'm surprised the news hasn't circulated yet, considering the number of neighbors who were peering out their windows and standing in their yards. My date was dead when I arrived there."

"What?" Wilson's eyes were huge.

I explained what had happened while Wilson alternately gaped at me and shook his head. "That is insane." He ran a hand through his white hair, making it stand up on end in spots.

I nodded, resisting the urge to reach out and smooth the hair down. "I hope the police chief was able to get in contact with Roger's other family members or that his sister did. I'd hate for his great-aunt Emily to come in here this morning and ask me the same question you did. She was so excited about our date, too," I added sadly.

Wilson asked, "Was his sister there last night?"

"She came by when she saw all the emergency vehicles. I think it probably scared her half to death. At any rate, it was a terrible evening, and I didn't get a lot of sleep last night, so I'll need to fire up the coffee maker in the breakroom," I said.

Wilson shifted uneasily, a gesture I'd come to know and dread.

"Uh-oh. What's wrong?" I asked, bracing myself against a bookcase. "Let me guess—the copier is jammed today. We're out of tax forms? The women's restroom is out of order? Even worse—the aforementioned *coffee maker* is broken? Don't hold back, I can take it."

"Worse," said Wilson gloomily. "Our new children's librarian is going to be late because of a family emergency."

"Don't tell me. You need me to do storytime today? Which one is scheduled this morning?"

"It's Mother Goose," said Wilson, referring to the toddler storytime. Usually the moms and kids were regaled with a great storyteller who used puppets and props to create a magical experience. This morning, on the other hand, we were all going to suffer through my rendition, involving last-minute prep and an overtired librarian.

"It's okay . . . I've got this," I said, trying to convince myself by sounding confident. "As long as it's not the adult craft class, right? You know how *that* turned out last time."

"The mosaics? Yes. The library board has decided you're banned in future from teaching craft-related programs," said Wilson dryly.

I winced at the memory. I'd been too gung-ho to think I could fill in for our program volunteer, who'd been out with the flu. In hindsight, we should simply have rescheduled the class. "Perhaps a less messy program would have been a better segue for me. Making wreaths, or something. Mother Goose storytime will be a cinch in comparison," I said.

"The bubbles are in the closet," said Wilson, with a chuckle.

"Bubbles, right." The toddlers were used to having bubbles blown at the start and end of storytime as a way of getting them into the mindset. I only hoped the bubble machine, finicky at the best of times, was in excellent working condition or the storytime couldn't possibly be redeemed.

"It's a nine o'clock event," said Wilson pointedly.

"And that's my cue," I said as I hurried off.

After I set up the books, bubble machine, and CDs in the community room, I walked over to the circulation desk to check out a patron who was having trouble with self-checkout. I saw a handwritten note on a scrap piece of paper on the desk. It read: *FYI, the cats belonged to Elsie Brennon. Unfortunately, she's recently deceased and the cats have no current home.* I glanced around the library as I handed the patron her books. I spotted Linus Truman, a regular, looking my way before he hastily glanced down at his book again. Despite the fact Linus was here every day, he never engaged with the librarians. It made sense if the note was from him . . . he wanted to help out, but didn't want to get pulled into conversation.

Then it was time for storytime. The amazing thing was that it went off much better than I could possibly have hoped. I knew the books would work well . . . I absolutely loved *Brown Bear, Brown Bear, What Do You See?* and *The Very Hungry Caterpillar*. The kids were adorable and the storytime itself was fun, if chaotic, with a roomful of toddlers. The only problem I usually had was with the moms. For some reason, this particular group of moms was very demanding, without a single laid-back mom in the group. This might be because they were a lot of first-time moms in the storytime. And if I wasn't completely prepared (as I wasn't this time) with not just books but songs and crafts, then the moms would let me know about it.

Before I joined the moms and toddlers who were already filling the room, I glanced back at our computer room hesitantly. Sure enough, there was a dad in there in with a toddler, same as there had been every day this week. He was waiting each morning when the library opened—said that he was job hunting because he'd lost his job last week.

I stuck my head through the glass doors of the room. He was focused on a job board while his little girl played with a doll on the floor next to him. "Hey, we're about to have storytime. Do you think your daughter might want to take part?"

He brightened. "That would be great. Except—I should be looking for jobs. I look in the morning and try to get to interviews in the afternoon."

"No problem. I can keep an eye on her for you," I said. I held out my hand to her, and she trustingly held onto it with her little hand. This definitely wasn't protocol. Library policy dictated each child should be accompanied by at least one caretaker. But that way the little girl could do something fun while her dad focused on finding work.

Somehow, I'd managed to get into the rhythm of the program this time. The bubble machine had gone off without a hitch and the toddlers danced around in delight, their little faces turned ecstatically up to the bubbles gently floating around them. The toddler girl from the computer room looked around in wonder at the bubbles, tentatively putting her hand out to touch any that came close.

I'd also pulled out an old CD player that was still loaded with a toddler CD and regaled the group with *The Wheels on the Bus* and *Head, Shoulder, Knees, and Toes.* We sang along together in between the books, which gave them the opportunity to move around and not have to sit still for too long. It is always good to get your wiggles out when you're a little kid.

I was just about to pull out a third book, the marvelous *Moo, Baa, La La La!*, when there was a tap at the glass door. I looked up and froze. There stood our friendly neighborhood vet from yesterday with two crates and two cats.

"Are those *cats*?" asked a tall mom, eyes narrowed, in the tone one might use to say *there are rabid coyotes in the building.*

Chapter Four

I winced. This was a mom who'd proven difficult to deal with in the past. She was a stickler for rules and had complained to the circulation desk before about various patrons who'd fallen asleep in the armchairs near the fireplace and people in the computer room who had drinks without lids on them.

All the mothers and most of the toddlers turned when the mom asked about the cats. In response, I quickly turned on the bubble machine and the CD player in the hopes of creating a massive distraction, excused myself, and stepped out of the room. Fortunately, the dad from the computer room showed up at that moment to collect his daughter.

"Thanks!" he said to me, gratitude in his eyes. "I've got a lead so I'm gonna call them and see if I can get an interview."

"Great! She loved storytime. And she was good as gold," I said.

As he took his daughter away, I sang out, "I'll be right back," to the women in the room behind me, not sure it was actually true.

"How are they doing?" I asked, stooping to peer into the crates one by one. I couldn't help myself—the sight of their little furry faces made me smile. The surprising thing was that both of them appeared very relaxed.

The vet grinned at me. "They are doing incredibly well. Your orange cat is the friendliest and most laid-back cat ever. And the tabby is such a sweetheart. They make me wish I didn't already have four cats of my own at home." She frowned. "It's still okay that I brought them here, isn't it?" She glanced at the group of moms through the door.

"Oh yes, it's fine. We'll keep them both here until we figure out what to do. A patron just told me they belonged to an elderly lady who'd died."

The vet nodded, "I didn't see any microchips, but they both seemed well-fed and healthy. And . . . a bonus! They both appear to be litter box trained."

"I believe I'd heard Mrs. Brennon was in a car accident a couple of weeks ago. They haven't been on their own for very long," I said.

"Medically, they're both in great shape. I've given them their shots and they're both fixed now. I guess their previous owner hadn't gotten around to doing that yet. The mama cat, because I do feel she's the orange cat's mother, will need to take it easy with her broken leg, but it set really well and I don't foresee any problems at all for her," said the vet.

"Perfect. Thank you. Here, I'll open the door to the lounge area and we'll keep the cats in here." I hesitated. "I really want to let the cats out when I can help them get acclimated. But I still need to wrap up my storytime. Could you leave the crates with me if I return them later?" I asked. I pushed some of my dark hair out of my eyes. Great. I was perspiring now.

"That's fine with me—I have a ton of them," said the vet. "Thanks again."

I walked back to the room and opened the door, giving everyone a flustered and apologetic grin. "Sorry about that," I started.

The tall mom again asked, "Hey, were those cats?"

I gave her a bright smile as if there were always cats populating the Whitby Library. "Indeed they were. Now, how about another song . . . and some bubbles?"

But even I could tell storytime was completely wrecked.

"Could we see the cats?" asked the mom. "By the way, I'm Lisa. I know we've talked before, but I don't think I've introduced myself."

I blinked at her. I'd assumed she'd been asking about the cats because she'd wanted to complain about them. "See them?"

A small, blonde mom said, "My daughter *loves* cats. Could you bring them into the room?"

I shook my head. "I'm sorry, but they've had a rough couple of days." I gave them a quick version of the cats' traumatic rescue. "And the vet has just brought them back from being fixed. The one cat has her leg set and needs to take it easy for a little bit."

Lisa said in a decisive tone, "You know what you should do? You should let them be library cats. Or at least one of them."

The blonde mom said to her, "Wouldn't that be so cool? The kids could cuddle with the cats and read stories to them. And it just sort of *fits* a library, doesn't it? So cozy. A cat, a bunch of books, and a fireplace. Sounds like heaven!"

"I don't think that's something the library is considering right now," I said evenly. But I felt my heart sink a little as I said it. Wilson was the boss, but I hoped he changed his mind about having a cat or two in the library. There was something about those two that really tugged at my heartstrings.

"You're looking for homes for them, then. Well, we'll consider one of them, for sure. The poor things. And we've been wanting to adopt an adult cat, too. Are they litter box trained?" asked Lisa briskly.

This was something I hadn't even considered . . . litter box training. And, with the way the blind date had gone last night, the cats had been forced out of my mind. At least I had a bit of litter and a smattering of food that the patron had brought in yesterday.

"The vet said they'd both used a litter box while they were at the vet's office last night. To be honest, we're not really set up with supplies here, at least, not many of them," I admitted. "The last twenty-four hours have been pretty chaotic."

Lisa didn't offer any judgement on my forgetfulness, but jumped into action. "Okay, here's what we're going to do. Janine, you can watch Sarah for me, right? I'm going to run to the store real quick and get you all set up."

"You don't have to do that," I said weakly, but she was already striding out of the room toward the library exit.

The blonde mom, who was apparently Janine, trundled little Sarah off to play with her son on the computers in the children's section. Storytime was effectively over and I hurried back to the lounge to see the cats.

I hoped they'd used their litter boxes recently because I wanted to let them out to slowly in the lounge to acclimate to their environment. But first I printed out a warning sign for the lounge door to say that the cats were on the loose and to be careful not to let them out. I had no intention of having them roam the library when they were in an unfamiliar place and might bolt.

Then I knelt down on the floor, crooning to the cats. Both of them seemed remarkably nonchalant about their current situation. I opened the door on the orange cat's crate first. He came out, purring and rubbing against me. Then he hopped up into my lap as I knelt and reached his head up to bump it against my neck. I couldn't help it . . . I was falling in love with this little guy.

Then I opened the door to the tabby's crate, and she came out with the same sangfroid, giving chatty little mews as she did. She walked a bit awkwardly with her leg in the cast, but seemed not to be in any pain at all.

Both cats strolled around the large room for several minutes. The lounge was a comfortable space with literary-themed posters, tables for librarians to eat snacks or their lunches, a small fridge and microwave, and some African violets on the sill of the large window that looked out on the library's front lawn. I made a quick online search to ensure the plants were safe for cats to be around and sighed with relief that they were. The cats, after sniffing and exploring, settled in the big sunbeam on the floor of the room. After licking themselves and each other for several minutes, they both curled up next to each other and drifted off to sleep.

At least, they drifted off until there was a peremptory knock at the door. I stifled a groan. The only person who'd knock at the door would be a patron, not a librarian. And that could mean anything could be wrong. I opened the door and saw Lisa there, holding several large bags. She'd apparently conscripted some male patron to help her unload her car, and he set down several large shopping bags of his own.

"Thank you!" said Lisa briskly, without turning to look at the man. She glanced at the empty crates and then immediately looked to the sunbeam. "Oh, they're just precious," she whispered.

The cats lifted their heads to look at her as if recognizing adoration when they heard it. The tabby cat struggled to her feet and then stumbled toward Lisa, purring.

Lisa hurried toward her so she didn't have to walk. "Oh my gosh. This cat is absolutely amazing! After all she's been through and she's this friendly? I'd be hiding in a corner somewhere if it had been me."

I smiled at her as I unpacked the plastic shopping bags. I saw Lisa had purchased dry and moist cat food, toys, beds, and another litter box. Whoever she was, she had a good heart. And, apparently, deep pockets.

"My husband and I have been planning to head to the shelter to find a cat for a while," said Lisa as she rubbed the tabby. "We just haven't gotten out there yet. This cat seems perfect. What can you tell me about her?"

I shook my head, "Not very much, I'm afraid. Just that the vet said she doesn't have any microchips. Another patron said the cats belonged to an elderly lady who recently passed away. The tabby had her shots and is fixed. I can tell you the tabby is supposed to stay quiet for a little while. She's likely the mother of the orange cat, according to the vet."

Lisa said, "I'm happy to reimburse the library for her medical care. I was wondering if my husband and I could take her home?" She looked at me with a hopeful look, the bossiness from earlier gone.

I hesitated to think it through for a minute. I knew Wilson wanted the cats out of the library, pronto. Lisa seemed as if she'd be a responsible pet owner—had, actually, already proven herself to be a responsible pet owner. And maybe it would be best for the cat to adjust to her forever home instead of getting used to the library only to be moved again. Besides, the tabby and Lisa appeared to be having a lovefest. The cat was in heaven as Lisa tickled her gently under her chin.

I smiled at her. "I think that would be perfect. And no worries about the vet bill—the vet did the work gratis. The only thing I need you to do is to return the crate to the vet when you can. The vet's name is written on the crate. And please take some of the cat equipment home."

"Thank you!" breathed Lisa. "I'm in here all the time, as you know, so I'll give you updates. And I'll give her a literary name that honors her history here."

"Great!" I said.

Wilson stuck his head in the door of the lounge and blinked in surprise at Lisa and the two cats. Lisa glanced up. "I'm on my way out, I promise. And I'm taking one of the cats off your hands, too."

"That's great," said Wilson in relief. He glanced down, bemused, at the orange cat sprawled out in a sunbeam. To me, he said, "The new children's librarian is here."

Excellent. "What is her name again?"

Wilson said, "Luna Macon. Could you do me a favor and show her around the library? I have a meeting I need to leave for."

I nodded and Wilson left.

Lisa gave the tabby another rub and then stood to push aside the blinds that gave the lounge area privacy from the rest of the library. "Wow," she said slowly. Then she grinned at me as she dropped the blinds back in place.

"Wow?" I asked weakly. I have always, always been wowed by children's librarians, but usually just in terms of how well they did their jobs.

Lisa said, "Let's just say I have the feeling storytime just got a little bit cooler. No offense."

"None taken," I responded automatically. I stood up too and pushed aside the blinds. There was a woman I'd never seen before, not in the town of Whitby, nor in the library. She had purple-streaked hair, a pierced nose, and sported black fingernail polish. There were tattoos peeking out from her black top (her black slacks were long enough to cover everything that might have poked out). I quickly dropped the blinds before she could turn and see me. Luna did look like she'd be bringing the cool factor to the Whitby Library.

"I'd better give my tour," I said quickly, giving Lisa a smile. I grabbed a piece of paper and a pencil and jotted out my name and phone number. "If you have any problems or any second thoughts at all about taking the tabby home, just call me. This is my cell number. If I'm at work, it may just take me a few minutes to get back to you."

Lisa took the paper, folded it, and put it in her pocket. "I'll keep this to keep you updated. But I know this little sweetie is a keeper."

I stepped out of the lounge and took a deep breath. I walked up to the middle-aged woman with a smile. "Luna Macon?" I asked.

She turned and bestowed me with the warmest, most genuine smile I'd ever seen. A gold tooth winked at me as she did. "That's right. You must be Ann. I'm *so* sorry about this morning and being a no-show. What a way to start a job, right?"

I said, "Don't worry about it. Believe me, it happens. Would you like me to show you around the library?"

"I'd love it," said Luna. "I haven't been here since I was a teenager and that's been a while, as you see." She laughed, and it was the infectious type that I couldn't help but respond to.

"Oh, did you grow up here?" I asked as we started walking toward the circulation desk.

She nodded. "Sure did. Then I moved away to—well, originally to New York, but then to a bunch of other places. Then back to New York. My mom is in poor health and that's why I'm back now. And why I was running late this morning." Although she was still smiling, I could see she looked tired and stressed.

With my first impression I'd wondered if maybe she'd stayed up too late partying the night before and then overslept because of a hangover. I was a little ashamed of myself for my leap to judgement. Despite all she seemed to be dealing with, she was warm and laid-back. Definitely more of an earth mother type. And kind, I thought as I spotted the twinkle in her eyes.

I gave Luna a quick tour of the library and helped get her acclimated. "The children's section is amazing, and it's really well-stocked. Nancy Drew was my favorite growing up and the Whitby Library has a huge collection of Nancys available for checkout. The patrons are terrific. And you'll never get bored. There hasn't been a day when I've worked here that I haven't been surprised by something." I figured this might be a good segue to telling her there was a cat in the lounge area. "Yesterday, for instance. Two boys came running in to ask for help rescuing two cats who were in a culvert outside in that rainstorm."

For the first time, Luna frowned. "Were they okay? The cats?"

I nodded. "One of them is still here. Heads-up that there's an orange cat hanging out in the breakroom. He seems really chilled out, actually, despite the fact he was in danger of drowning yesterday and got fixed by a vet last night."

"And the other cat?" asked Luna.

"One of our storytime moms jumped into action and bought a slew of stuff for the cats. She ended up taking the tabby home—the vet said the tabby was most likely the orange cat's mom," I said.

"Sounds like I've got a cool group for storytime," said Luna with a slow-spreading grin. Then she raised her eyebrows.

"Uh-oh. Don't look now, but it looks like you're wanted by the cops."

Chapter Five

I turned and saw Burton Edison approaching me. He blinked briefly in surprise at Luna's general appearance before giving her a hesitant smile.

"Could you just give me a few minutes?" I asked. Luna gave the chief a saucy wink which made him color slightly, and then she headed off in the direction of the children's section.

"Hi, Chief Edison," I said.

"Call me Burton," he said immediately. "Hope you're having a quieter day than you did yesterday." His eyes followed Luna as she disappeared into the children's section.

Despite the fractured storytime and the sudden appearance of the vet, it *was* a quieter day. Which was quite a testament to how crazy yesterday had been. I nodded. "Do you have any news on what happened to Roger?" I asked quietly. Not because I was trying to be especially quiet in our library, which was always filled with happy chatter except in the study zone. But because voices tended to carry there. Something to do with the acoustics of the old place.

Burton gave a wry chuckle. "If only. No, it's probably going to take us a while to get to the bottom of this one. But I was driving by the library and thought I'd pop in so we could finalize the details of the self-defense class."

I nodded, pulling out the library event calendar app I kept on my phone. "Didn't you want to do it sooner rather than later? We have a canceled event in a couple of days and the community room is available after five. That would be Monday. I know that's short notice and you might need more time to prepare. Or, you know, the murder investigation might be taking a big chunk of your time."

Burton said, "A self-defense class is something I could do in my sleep, fortunately. That will work out fine. I've got to keep somewhat regular hours, even with an investigation going on. Believe me, I'm no good without meals, sleep, and downtime. Let's do it then."

I hesitated. "I hate for you to waste your time. I know you must be really busy trying to ramp up into your job. And I'm not sure how high attendance will be since I won't be able to put the word out for very long."

"No problem. Even if there are just one or two attendees, it'll be worth my time. It's something I feel pretty passionately about," said Burton. He hesitated. "While I'm here, there's something I'd like to bounce off of you."

"Sure thing," I said. I gestured over to a nearby table and chairs. "Do you want to sit down?"

We took a seat. Burton said, "I noticed you spent a little time speaking with Roger Wilson's sister, Heather. I don't mind telling you that when it was time for us to talk, she really buttoned her lips. I don't know if she's just not fond of the police or what, but all I could get out of her was that Roger was a devoted brother."

I said, "Maybe that's all there was to their relationship. She said much the same to me."

"But here's the thing. I know he's a single guy. So am I. But in my house, I've got family pictures up. Some of them are pictures my mom gave me or my sister-in-law. I have Christmas cards up and whatnot. And on my fridge, there are hand-drawn pictures of me as a stick man with a big head that my little niece and nephew drew. Me—as a stick man!" Burton looked ruefully down at his solid frame.

"I see what you're getting at. So, for Roger to be such a devoted brother, you'd think there'd be some sort of evidence of that in his house," I said. "Things that show he interacted with them and celebrated holidays with them."

Burton nodded.

"I wish I could tell you more about their relationship," I said slowly. "But although I've seen Heather pretty frequently at the library in the past, I don't really know her. And I didn't know Roger at all. But I can tell you that Heather said there was someone who might have been especially upset with Roger. Apparently one of his former coworkers blamed him for her not getting a promotion. And then she was fired or let go or something, and she somehow thought he was complicit in that, too."

Burton had his notebook out and was making notes in a very neat handwriting. "Can you remember this woman's name?"

I thought about this for a second. "Mary, I think. I can't remember her last name, but she works over at the tanning salon in the strip mall."

Burton raised his eyebrows. "Considering we know Roger was an investment counselor, that seems like a pretty big step down in salary. No wonder she's feeling bitter. Okay, thanks for this. I'll follow up on that." He tapped his pencil on the notepad. "One other question. Are you familiar at all with a Nathan Richardson?"

I frowned. "Yes, I know him really well. Is he all right?"

Burton immediately adopted a calming demeanor. "I'm sure he's fine. I've just got a few questions for him, that's all. It seems he might have had an altercation with the deceased. Does that sound likely?"

"Not at *all*," I said. "He was my English professor and we still keep in touch. In fact, I visit him just about every week. I can't imagine him having an altercation with anyone. Do you have more information?"

He closed his notebook and quickly said, "Not really. It's just something I have to check into." Clearly, this was the end of the questions about Nathan. I felt a knot in my stomach. I'd have to get in touch with him and see what was going on.

Burton glanced over at the stacks and spotted a book. He got up from our table and walked over to pick out a World War II military history, Rick Atkinson's *An Army at Dawn*.

"Good choice," I said, nodding at the book. "It's really well-written."

"Is it?" asked Burton, thumbing through it.

"It won the Pulitzer, actually. And it's part of a trilogy, so if you like it, there are two more volumes here," I said.

He nodded again. "I like to read before I fall asleep at night. Mostly nonfiction."

"This should be right up your alley. Do you have a library card?" I asked.

He flushed and then gave an awkward laugh. "Nope! I guess I was just going to walk out of here with it. Some chief of police I am."

I smiled at him. "It's okay to be absent-minded when you have as much going on as you do right now. I'll get you a card. It'll take just a couple of minutes, I promise." Once again, I remembered how I'd pegged him as the backwoods, backwards small-town cop and shook my head. Burton, despite his appearance, was clearly anything but.

He cleared his throat as I got him registered for a library card and checked his book out. "Your librarian there. She's very different from most of the residents I've seen here in Whitby."

"Luna? She just started here today. She's apparently not been in Whitby for a while, but her mom lives here, and she's taking care of her while she's under the weather."

He said slowly, "So she's only here temporarily?"

"Actually, no. At least, not as far as I understand. She's our new children's librarian, and it's not supposed to be a temporary position," I said.

I was a little confused as to why Burton was so interested. Did he think Luna looked like a person of interest in a case? Did he think she might be trouble? But then I saw his gaze following her as she walked to the computer area. Was he interested in Luna . . . romantically? I hid a smile. I'd never have put the two of them together. He looked like the personification of law and order and Luna looked like a free spirit. I noticed he looked away hurriedly when he saw I'd been watching him.

"Thanks for this," he said in a hurry, waving the book in the air. "See you soon."

I nodded absently, still thinking I needed to get the word out for the class. Even though Burton didn't seem to mind the idea of teaching a class with low attendance, I sure didn't want to be the only one who showed up.

Luna walked up to me, smiling. "That orange cat is *amazing*, by the way. What's the plan with him? Are we looking for a home for him?"

"Do you need a cat?" I asked hopefully. "Or does your mom?"

Luna laughed. "I wish I could take him! My mom loves cats, but has her hands full with the one she has. Plus, he's not a cat that plays well with others. And I'm living with my mom. If I weren't, I'd love to take him."

"I hope Wilson changes his mind about keeping him. I think he'd make an awesome addition to the library."

"What's he worried about?" asked Luna with a frown.

"I just don't think he's all that much into animals," I said. "And I think he's worried that having a cat here might make for problems. At any rate, I'm going to put up some flyers with the cat and see if we can find him a good home."

Luna said, "I bet he'll change his mind. That cat is like a ragdoll . . . he's going to curl up next to patrons or on patrons and make everybody's collective stress level go way down." She glanced outside and saw Burton getting in his car. "Say, if you don't mind me asking, what was the deal with the cop?"

Sadly, Burton didn't seem to be on Luna's radar in a romantic sense. Pity.

I took a deep breath in order to answer her question. "Yesterday was a pretty awful day." I quickly filled Luna in on what had happened after I left the library.

She gave a low whistle. "That's the worst date I've ever heard of. Are you okay?"

"I'm fine—it was just a shock. I'm more worried about Roger's family. And maybe the folks who've come under suspicion." My mind went back to my old professor. I said, "I'm sorry, I think I need to make a quick phone call. And shouldn't you be on your lunch break?"

Luna squinted at the wall clock. "Yikes. See ya later." And she scurried off in the direction of the lounge.

I stepped into the stacks for a minute to make a surreptitious call. Nathan picked right up.

"Ann?" he asked.

"Hey there," I blurted. "Listen, I'm at work, but I just wanted to check in with you really quick. Have you . . . well, are you familiar with Roger Walton at all?"

There was a pause on the other end and then Nathan's voice, sounding tired. "I'm afraid so. And I think I know why you're checking on me. The police chief called me this morning and wants to speak with me this afternoon. I heard about Roger's death. But Ann, I had nothing to do with it."

The stress in his voice gave me a pang. "Of course you didn't," I said fiercely. "Nobody could possibly think you did."

This was the same man who'd gotten his classes to memorize and recite the prologue to *The Canterbury Tales* in middle English. It was completely impossible that he'd stabbed someone with a grill skewer.

He gave a wry chuckle. "I'm very much afraid they could, Ann. At any rate, I can fill you in later today after I've spoken with him. Why don't you come over for supper? Say around 6:30, if you're free?"

This was a regular thing for us. He'd invite me over for supper to his house—and I'd always offer to bring Chinese takeaway. That's because his cooking since his wife died had tended towards frozen pizza and microwave meals, but also because Chinese food was his favorite.

"That sounds perfect." I hesitated. "Maybe you should ask a lawyer to be there with you. Just to be on the safe side."

Nathan said gently, "I have nothing to hide. Although, unfortunately, I also don't have an alibi since I live alone. Unless Mr. Henry can offer one."

I heard a little yip in the background from the little Yorkshire terrier as he heard Nathan say his name. I smiled. "I'll see you both at 6:30."

I hung up and stretched to get the stress out of my shoulders. I'd always been fond of Nathan, even as a student. But after my aunt died a few years ago, he'd become almost like my surrogate grandfather. I didn't want him to be a suspect in a murder investigation.

The rest of the hour until my lunch break was spent with a patron who was a computer novice and was trying to research a particular type of cancer her sister had. I was able to pull up some reliable sources for her from the National Cancer Institute and the American Cancer Society, printing them out so she could read through them later. Then I walked into the breakroom to grab both my lunch and my purse. Usually I ate lunch at the library, but today I had a different plan.

Luna was walking out as I was walking in and gave me a wink. I glanced, confused, into the room and saw Wilson sitting in a chair with the orange cat purring like crazy in his lap.

I hastily hid a smile and acted as if it wasn't a totally astonishing scene.

Wilson said gruffly, "Why haven't you picked out a name for this cat? It's ridiculous to keep calling it 'cat' or 'orange cat.' It makes me feel about five years old."

"Well, I was trying to avoid getting too *attached* to the cat," I said. "Under the circumstances."

"What circumstances are those?" asked Wilson, glowering at me.

I swear sometimes he made me feel as if I was the one losing my mind with his swift about-faces. "Where we're finding a good home for him."

"No, no. We're not doing that. This cat will be pure marketing gold, Ann. Gold, I'm telling you." The orange cat reached up and bumped his head lovingly under Wilson's chin.

I opened my mouth and then just shut it again. Wilson seemed to be on a roll.

"What I need you to do is to find out what we can do to help eliminate the whole allergy problem," said Wilson.

I nodded, getting my lunch out of the fridge.

"No, really. Can you do that now?" asked Wilson.

I plopped down and pulled out my phone. "I'm on it." A few minutes later I said, "It looks like vacuuming with a HEPA filter really helps. This article also mentions removing carpet and drapes. But we've already done that." Wilson had gone on a renovation spree a few years back and had had the old, stained carpeting ripped up and the curtains taken down. It made things a bit louder, but the general effect was one of a well-lit, comfortable space.

"Anything else?" he asked.

"Filters. Filters on the vents are useful, as well, according to the article." I put my phone away and started walking to the door, pointedly, with my lunch.

Wilson was apparently still lost in his own world. A world revolving around felines. "And the name? He needs to have a name."

"How about, when I get back from lunch, if I get the patrons involved in the process?" I asked, giving the door a longing look.

Wilson snapped his fingers. "A contest. We'll make it a contest and put up flyers in the library and posts on social media. It's all about engagement, Ann. We need to keep the community *engaged*."

"It's a perfect idea, Wilson," I said. "I'll get right on it."

I hurried out the door with a relieved sigh. When Wilson got on a roll, there was no telling what would end up on my to-do list. And right now, I had something else I wanted to do. I wanted to meet Mary, Roger's former coworker. I knew she was also now on Burton's list of people to talk with, but my talk would be a lot more casual. I didn't want to get on Mary's radar as a problem. I hopped in my car, taking a few bites of my pimento cheese sandwich.

Chapter Six

Whitby was not a big town, so I knew exactly where the tanning salon was, despite never having been there. It was in a strip of older shops that wasn't exactly the town's best feature. The rest of Whitby looked like something out of a Chamber of Commerce catalog: carefully preserved old buildings, a picturesque town square with an interesting historic statue of a bespectacled man waving his arms about, and a wide boulevard of a main street dotted with businesses and beautiful old homes.

On the way over I managed to eat most of my lunch. I was used to eating quickly anyway, since sometimes the other library staff would need my help and interrupt my lunch break. Besides, it wasn't exactly the type of lunch you cared to linger over, savoring every bite. I parked in front of the tanning salon, rather uncreatively named 'Suntastic' and walked in the door.

There was only one employee there, and I hoped she was Mary Hughes. She was a short woman of about fifty who was a little heavy and sported a great tan. I suddenly realized how very pale I must look in comparison. Her blonde hair had the look of being dyed and her brown eyes seemed bored. She had a manicure that needed touching-up.

"Can I help you?" she asked in a voice that sounded as bored as her expression.

I said, "Hi there. I just wanted to pick up some information about tanning. And a price list."

The woman pulled out a brochure. "Here's what we have. If you have any other questions, you can give me a call. I'm usually here."

I saw that she wrote down *Mary* on the brochure and circled the phone number for the salon.

"Thanks," I said. I hesitated, not really having expected this meeting to take so little time.

Mary shrugged and appeared to be trying to drum up some interest. "Are you thinking of tanning for a special occasion, or were you wanting it to be a regular thing? There are discount packages listed in there if you want to come more than just a handful of times." She glanced at my skin. "You're gonna have to be real careful not to get yourself burned in one of those beds. Looks like you haven't exactly spent a ton of time in the sun."

"No reunion or wedding or anything like that. I was thinking about making some personal changes and this is something I've had on my mind for a while," I lied. I knew there was one thing I definitely was *not* interested in and that was tanning. I'd realized when I was a kid that someone with my dark hair, blue eyes, and porcelain skin didn't really *tan*. What we did instead was burn to a crisp. "I had kind of an upsetting day yesterday and it made me rethink my priorities."

I hoped that didn't sound lame. Apparently, it didn't to Mary, who now showed the first sign of piqued interest.

"What happened to you yesterday?" she asked, tilting her head to one side. Then she appeared to remember her manners. "That is, if you don't mind talking about it. Although I've found that sometimes talking about stuff makes it easier," she said persuasively.

Mary, from my experience working with the public for years, seemed to be the type who thrived on gossip. I swore her pupils dilated at the prospect of hearing something that could be scandalous. I lowered my voice, as if anyone else was in the building, and said, "I had a blind date that went really, really wrong. I mean, blind dates are rough anyway, right? But this one was the worst. I showed up to his house at the time we were supposed to meet and he didn't answer the door. I could smell the grill going, so I walked around the side of the house to see if he was outside. That's when I found him. Dead."

Mary jerked back in surprise. "Roger Walton."

I said slowly, "You knew him? And knew about his death?"

Mary said, "That's right." She added quickly, "My coworker called me last night pretty late. I used to work with him and she knew that and called to let me know." Mary narrowed her eyes. "Before I say anything, did *you* know him? You said it was a blind date, right? So you hadn't even met him? Weren't fond of him?"

I shook my head.

Mary nodded. "Okay. Well, the truth is I didn't like the guy at all. I think you had a lucky escape . . . uh, what was your name?"

"Ann Beckett."

"Ann, you had a lucky escape," said Mary with a short laugh.

I said, since I wasn't supposed to know their connection, "You were in a relationship with him?"

Mary shook her head emphatically. "No way. I'm a lot older than he is, anyway. No, we worked together. Not here at the tanning salon, of course. That was when I had my more professional job as an investment counselor. Bet you couldn't tell I'm a whiz at stocks and bonds, could you?" Her voice was bitter, but the kind of bitter with a lot of sadness rolled into it.

"You were coworkers, then?" I asked.

"Yep. And at first it seemed like everything was fine. He was friendly enough and could be good for a laugh. But he was also sort of a slacker. I'd be working my fingers to the bone, and I'd look over and he'd be on his phone on a personal call or just pushing papers around on his desk. I didn't think he put a lot of time into the company. And I didn't think he was as good with investments or gave as good advice as I did. But, after all, I'd been with the company a lot longer than he was," Mary said.

I said, "He sounds like he'd be tough to have as a coworker."

She shrugged. "He was all right. Until one of the managers retired, and the company wanted to promote from within. I *knew* I was going to get the promotion. There was no way I *couldn't* get it. I put in longer hours than Roger did, I'd been there way longer, I'd paid my dues, and I was just better at the job. But the next thing I know, Roger has this hush-hush, door shut meeting with our boss. And then *he* ended up with the promotion! I tell you, the guy had a golden tongue."

I said, "So you think he was in there flattering the boss? Talking his way into the job?"

"It was probably partly that, but mostly that he was sabotaging *me*. I think he went in there with some sort of made-up story about my incompetence so I'd be sure not to get the manager position," said Mary. A vein pulsed on the side of her forehead at the memory.

I said slowly, "That must have made you furious."

Mary said, "I was livid. I'd worked really hard there and finally had an opportunity to advance. It's not a big firm, but it's well-respected enough that people come from other towns. And the employees stay there forever, so there hadn't been any chance to move up the ladder with the managers sticking around until they retired."

"You think you'd have gotten the manager position if Roger hadn't persuaded them not to give it to you?"

"No question," said Mary.

"Did you quit because of that? Did you end up so angry with the company that you decided to work somewhere else entirely?" I asked curiously. Because it seemed like a strange thing to do. Wouldn't it have been better to simply suck it up and stay at the same place, making a better salary?

Mary shrugged again, not seeming eager to give her reasons behind her current employment. "Let's just say I didn't leave as much as I was forced out."

"Just the same, I'd think you'd *still* be furious," I said. "You said you were livid before and I wouldn't think it would get easier over time."

Mary said, "My mother always said to let bygones be by-gones. I managed to let it go." But there was a glitter in her eyes that made me think maybe she wasn't as laid-back about Roger's interference in her promotion as she seemed.

I changed tack. "The police didn't seem to have a lot of information about what happened. I didn't see anything that would help them out, either. I wish I had." I paused, hoping Mary would chime in with information of her own.

But Mary immediately shook her head. "I didn't see any-thing either. I was stuck here working an evening shift yesterday. People like to come after work to do their tanning, so I'm fre-quently here."

I nodded. Then I said, "I guess I'm just really curious be-cause I was supposed to go on a date with the guy. I can't help but wonder what happened to him and why."

Mary said, "Look, I get it. That's human nature, right? You're curious. But here's the deal: Roger was a miserable per-son. Like I said, you had a lucky escape. In my opinion, Roger was a real snake in the grass. Here's how I think the first date would have gone—he'd have charmed you to death."

This wasn't what I'd expected her to say. "He would have?"

"Right. He was good at that. So, he'd have been engaging in really interesting conversation and given you a number of cool stories about his life. Maybe they'd even have been made up, but they'd all have served the purpose to be charming," said Mary. "He'd have tried to suck you in."

"And then?" I asked, curious in spite of myself. I didn't par-ticularly like how Mary assumed I could be easily sucked in.

"Then, later, after you two had an established relationship, the real Roger would have started slipping out through the cracks. The guy who was ridiculously ambitious and greedy and self-centered and irresponsible and not there for his family. Everything was about Roger," said Mary.

I nodded, hoping she'd continue ranting about Roger because I was getting a better picture of him—or at least, her perspective of him. "What were you saying about his family? I know he had a sister."

Mary rolled his eyes. "Oh, he wasn't even nice to his family. I know his sister couldn't stand him."

"Really?" That's certainly not the impression Heather had given when she was talking like a devoted sister.

"Really. I don't know all the details, mind you. Only that he'd get into shouting matches with her in the office . . . he'd have to walk out to continue the argument because it would get too heated. No, he was just useless all around," said Mary.

"Do you think someone in his family could be responsible?" I asked.

Mary held up a hand. "Now, like I say, I don't know all the details. Just that he didn't get along with some of his family. I'm not saying they were out to kill him. No, if someone wanted to kill him, I'd put my money on this one guy."

At this point, the bell on the door rang, and a woman came in for tanning. Mary signed her in and took her to the back while I waited impatiently for her to return and tell me who she thought might be angry enough at Roger to kill him. Besides, my lunch hour was rapidly running out.

Mary returned and frowned. "What was I saying?"

"That you'd put money on somebody to have murdered Roger. Some guy."

Mary snapped her fingers. "That's right. There was this investor who followed Roger's advice. Roger could really lay it on when he recommended investments, but like I said, he wasn't great at his job."

"So he recommended some investments that didn't perform well?" I asked.

"Exactly. Roger always made them sound like the best thing since ice cream. He was a great salesman, I have to admit. Or maybe just a good actor. He'd start telling someone about something he knew about that was too good to be true. Of course, later it would end up it was *too* good to be true. Roger would play it up like he was doing the client a favor, and they'd always go for it."

"How did those investments end up working out?" I asked.

Mary shrugged. "They'd work out on a range from mediocre to appalling. But you've got to understand most people never really even check their investments much. They could be bleeding cash and be tied up in all kinds of high fees and they never know it because they never take a look. Anyway, this older guy was different. Sharp as a tack, I think. He followed Roger's advice and lost a ton of money. Apparently, he'd put a lot of his retirement savings into those investments and he was not young," said Mary.

"But isn't that the nature of investing?" I asked with a frown. Besides a few piddly retirement investments, I wasn't exactly playing the stock market. "Don't you assume there's some risk involved?"

"Sure, but sometimes there's more risk involved than others. And usually you choose less-risky investments when you're closer to retirement age. And Roger *always* oversold everything he dealt with. He made everything sound like something too good to pass up. This guy should have been advised to put his money in something safe, not some risky get-rich-quick scheme," said Mary.

"Do you remember who the investor was?" I asked.

Mary said, "Well, usually we wouldn't give out that kind of information since financial-related stuff is private. But seeing as how I got shafted at the firm, I can tell you the investor was Nathan Richardson."

My heart sank. I was hoping the 'elderly investor' was someone else, instead of my former professor.

"You know him?" asked Mary, eyes narrowed.

"I do. Poor guy. I didn't realize that had happened to him," I said slowly.

"That's pretty amazing, considering the fact the guy talks about it to just about everyone," said Mary dryly. "For a while he was threatening to sue the firm. He wouldn't have gotten far, of course, considering we all know investments come with a certain amount of risk attached."

I said, "I'm kind of surprised, though, that the investment firm didn't fire Roger over something like this. It sounds as if he was really imprudent in the way he advised Nathan."

Mary shrugged. "That's what I'm saying. Roger could get away with murder. The upper-management probably discounted the older guy's complaints."

"They shouldn't have done that. Nathan is incredibly bright and well-spoken," I said.

"Well, that's clearly what they did. And then Roger probably talked his way out of getting any kind of reprimand by misrepresenting what he told his investor," said Mary.

The door chimed again and Mary gave me an impatient look.

I raised my brochure. "Thanks again for the information . . . and for the talk."

She didn't answer. She was already chatting to the customer.

Chapter Seven

The library was bustling when I returned. I checked in on Luna, who gave me a thumbs-up from the children's section where she was expertly giving advice to a mom who wanted to find books similar to the Harry Potter series. I could hear Luna's animated voice as she compared *Percy Jackson and the Olympians* and the *Ranger's Apprentice* series with the Harry Potter books.

I still had a few minutes left on my lunch hour, so I headed to the lounge to check on the orange cat and to finish off the last few bites of my lunch. As soon as I opened the door, he made a trilling noise and jumped to his feet to wind himself lovingly around my legs.

I sat on the floor and he crawled into my lap, bumping his head against my neck. "What a sweetie," I said to him, rubbing him under his neck as his whiskers quivered with delight. "We're going to come up with a great name for you so we don't have to keep calling you orange cat."

The cat pulled his head back to stare piercingly at me with his beautiful green eyes. It was almost as if he knew what I was saying. For the next few minutes, I sat with him and loved on him and felt my stress level plummet. He really was the sweetest cat ever. Then, I gave him a final rub and got to my feet to finish off my lunch. He watched me intently as I finished my grapes. I looked in the bag of supplies that the storytime mom had dropped off for the cat. Sure enough, she'd forgotten nothing. I pulled out a bag of cat treats and gave him a few.

Remembering Wilson's edict to set up a cat naming contest, I pulled out my phone and took a few pictures of the orange cat who was now lying on his back and grinning lazily up at my phone, I picked the best one and made up a quick flyer on the breakroom computer, then printed copies and put them all over the library to advertise our 'name the cat' contest. I put it on all the library social media sites, too.

Then I figured I could use the cat to announce the self-defense class. Not that one had anything to do with the other, and it was a totally gratuitous use of the cat, but a cute picture might get in front of more patrons on social media than otherwise. The orange cat was now dozing, snoring lightly, and I took a picture and posted the self-defense class info with a header saying "Don't be caught napping! Learn self-defense moves on Monday with Whitby's new sheriff!" I made a face. It was corny, but maybe it would get some shares. The cat looked adorable after all.

Once I left the breakroom, I helped a patron figure out how to find some genealogical information on her family and she was pleased to find out how much information was available online (and for free). Then a patron asked me to help her set up a new email address because her old one was overrun with spam. I showed her how to send a group email to let all of her contacts know about the email address change. I shelved some books, added books that had been requested by patrons to the holds shelf, and then talked with some folks who were coming up with names for the cat. So far, we seemed overrun with Kitty, Max, Milo, Tigger, and Felix. It was a good thing it was a contest and not a vote. The mild-mannered orange cat wouldn't be the type to mind *any* name, but I kind of hoped for something more original for him.

Finally, there was a lull in the library while the patrons were all focused on the book, periodical, or computer they were looking at. Luna walked up to me.

"How's it going?" I asked. For me, first days had always been stressful. But Luna looked as comfortable as if she'd been in the Whitby Library all of her life.

"It's great. I love the patrons here. The parents have been terrific and the kids have been adorable. I felt good about helping them find a new series or picture books and the library has an awesome collection, just like you said. I'm looking forward to the storytime this afternoon," said Luna.

"Good," I said. "Do you have any questions for me at all?"

She grinned at me. "As a matter of fact, I do. What's the status of the orange cat? I saw he and Wilson were looking very cozy with each other in the breakroom."

I grinned back at her. "Apparently, we now have ourselves a library cat."

Luna gave a whoop. "I hoped so! I spotted one of your flyers and thought it would stink if we had to give him away after coming up with a name for him. That's awesome! That cat could win anybody over."

"Now we just have to figure out a name for him," I said dryly.

Luna asked, "While you were out at lunch, did you hear any news updates? You know, about your date?"

I said with a smile, "You've been away from Whitby for a while. We don't really have that kind of news coverage here. It's definitely going to make the newspaper, but it's not on radio or TV or anything."

"Oh, right." Luna made a face. "I'm just curious."

I glanced around, but no one was within earshot or needed help. I said, "But I did go to the salon where Mary, Roger's former coworker works."

Luna's eyes opened wide. "Find out anything?"

"She definitely wasn't happy with Roger, that's for sure. She admitted she felt he'd cut her out of a promotion, although she was a little cagier about how she ended up at the tanning salon. But she says she was working at the time Roger would have been murdered, so I suppose she has an alibi."

Luna said, "Well, naturally that's what she's going to say. But honestly, who'd notice if she stepped out for a few minutes to knock him off? It's not like the tanning salon has a line out the door, does it?"

I considered this. "True. And the salon is actually very close to Roger's house, if she were willing to cut through some private property to get there. The problem I have with it is . . . why now? I'd think if you were unhappy about getting let go, you'd commit murder right after you were let go. I'm thinking a few weeks or a month has gone by. Mary already has a tan from the salon. Why not just get revenge on Roger right away, right after she'd lost her job?"

Luna shrugged. "Maybe it just festered for a while like a wound that doesn't heal. Or maybe now the layoff is really hitting hard. Maybe she's developed a health problem and her current insurance isn't good. Maybe she's just miserable at her job and is angry she's not an investment counselor anymore."

I said slowly, "Or maybe she thought getting rid of Roger right after she was laid off would make her too much of a suspect."

"There you go again! Your deductions are right on, Nancy Drew" said Luna.

I said, "I probably need to fill in the police chief."

Luna shrugged. "Sure. But isn't he doing some sort of self-defense thing here on Monday? I saw it on the social media feed. You could just tell him then. So who's the next suspect? Did you get any leads on who else had a beef with Roger?"

I hesitated and then slowly said, "Mary said there was an investor who was upset with Roger for some bad advice he'd given him. Apparently, he'd lost a lot of money."

"Did she give you a name?" asked Luna.

"She did. And I actually know him. He's a friend of mine—he was one of my college professors. There's absolutely no way he could have done it. He's never displayed temper, ever. He never even raised his voice in class. He was an amazing teacher, and he's always been so patient and kind. He's one of those types of people who always has a twinkle in his eye."

"Sure, but keeping your cool in a classroom and keeping your cool during a bad financial transaction are two different things. You know how people can be when it comes to money. Nobody wants their standard of living to go down," said Luna.

"It has to be someone else. It sounds like Roger might have been the kind of person to make a lot of people angry."

Luna leaned forward. "You know most murders are committed by someone the victim knew. Or family. What's this guy, Roger's, family like?"

"I did have a chance to talk to his sister for a while. She indicated they had a good relationship," I said.

"Naturally she's going to say that. But what impression did you get from her?" asked Luna.

I thought about this for a moment. "Honestly, I felt like I wasn't hearing the whole story. And for such a devoted brother, the police chief thought it was weird he didn't have pictures of Heather or her child up."

Luna said. "Makes sense to me. Now, on to another subject. What do you do here in Whitby when you're *not* at the library? I need some ideas. I'm pretty locked down with my mom right now, but I want to have some good plans for when she's back on her feet."

I snorted. "When I'm *not* at the library? Is this a trick question?"

"Oh, come on! You're young and attractive. You seem fun. You've got to be doing more with your time than working here, reading, and finding dead bodies," said Luna dryly.

I blew out a deep breath and tried to think. "Yeah, I do some stuff, but it's probably not the normal activities of your usual thirty-something. I run sometimes . . . although I've gotten off-track with that lately. I like to go hiking on the Blue Ridge Parkway trails. Occasionally, I'll be part of the local theater—they have an amateur production company that is fun. And then I re-place the birdseed at the park on Thursdays."

I stopped this rendition as Luna gave me a horrified look. "Note to self," she said, "Find Ann some fun things to do."

I heard someone calling my name and turned around to see Roger's Great-Aunt Emily walking toward me. She had tears in her eyes and was clearly distressed.

"I should get back to work," murmured Luna. "Talk later."

I gave Emily a quick hug, and she clung onto me as if for dear life. "Oh, Ann!" she moaned.

"How are you holding up?" I asked, pulling back to take a look at her. "Let's sit over here and have a talk."

We walked over to sit down in the cozy armchairs near the fireplace and the periodicals. I was glad for Emily to sit down. Whether from her tears or distress, she was wobbling unsteadily on her feet. The last thing I needed was another emergency on my hands.

Emily visibly tried to pull herself together, blinking her eyes and dabbling at them with a torn tissue. She sighed and said, "As I was trying to say, I'm so sorry you had to go through that yesterday, Ann! How awful it must have been for you; you were thinking you were going out for a fun evening and then . . ." She gave a great, shuddering sigh. "I feel so very terrible. I engineered this entire situation! I should never have tried matchmaking. It's just that I have so much time on my hands and not enough to do."

"Don't worry about me," I said, giving her hand a quick squeeze. "I promise you, I'm fine. It was a terrible evening. But I can't imagine how you must be feeling, trying to cope with your nephew's death. That must have been such an awful shock for you."

Emily nodded, an exhausted expression on her face. "It was. I think it's really just now settling in. I couldn't believe Roger was gone and in such a violent way. It's so very disturbing. Heather called me as soon as she could to let me know."

"Yes, I saw Heather last night at Roger's house," I said slowly. "I felt bad for her."

"And there don't seem to be any leads to tell us what happened," said Emily sadly. "It just seems like the perpetrator disappeared into thin air. It's so unfair to Roger—just starting out with a life of his own. And poor Heather—it must have been such a shock for her. Although, you know, Heather is just a rock; she is so organized and amazing. I think she keeps her emotions in check. Then the emotions come out sometime later and ambush her."

I nodded. "I'm like that too, sometimes. It's fine to keep your feelings inside . . . until one day when the dam breaks when you least expect it."

Emily sighed. "She's such a good girl, you know. She took care of her mother for years when she was suffering from cancer. I don't know how she did it with a job and a baby in tow. I tried to help her out when I could, but the truth is I just didn't have the stamina for it. But all the radiation and chemo treatments seemed to work, finally! We were so grateful. She's in remission now, bless her. She decided the house and yard were too much for her, so Heather found a good retirement community for her to move to. It was quite a job, too. Heather helped her pack up some things and had a yard sale for the rest." She sighed. "If only she could have had some help. If Roger could have maybe driven her to chemo treatments and that sort of thing."

"Perhaps he was too busy with work?" I asked.

Emily apparently wasn't the type to speak ill of the dead. "I'm sure he wanted to help. But you know how some men are."

Not particularly. Not when it came to not helping out with a family emergency. But I nodded at Emily to encourage her to continue.

"He would pop by from time to time. He always made his mother laugh and that would cheer her up for a while. But I think it really troubled him to see her like that."

I bobbed my head again in understanding although I was becoming increasingly glad that I hadn't had that date with Roger. I'm sure it also troubled Heather to see her mother 'like that,' but she was able to move past it and help to nurse her.

Emily continued as if needing to come up with additional excuses for Roger's slack behavior. "He also had a lot of things going on at his office at the time his mother was sick. There was some sort of flap with a fellow employee that he talked about a lot. Apparently, she was a real piece of work. The office was good to get rid of her." She paused. "I'm sure he did help to a certain degree. He probably advised Heather on the business aspects of the sale. He was wonderful at business. It's just a pity he was taken from us so soon."

Roger had not even been dead for 24 hours and I'd yet to hear anyone say really wonderful, glowing things about him. Even his great-aunt Emily was struggling to find something other than 'wonderful at business.'

But Emily looked so tired and dispirited that I wanted to try to distract her for at least a few minutes. She'd been a regular patron at the library since far before I started, and she was always cheerful and made me smile when she was here.

"Again, I'm so sorry about Roger. I know the police are working very hard to find who's responsible for his death."

She reached out and briefly squeezed my hand. "Thank you. You're such a calming influence, Ann." She laughed. "And I promise I won't set you up on another date again. My matchmaking days are over. I'll just have to figure out another way to spend them. Solitaire? Crosswords?"

I frowned and then said slowly, "I think you actually live in my neighborhood, don't you, Emily?"

She nodded and I continued, "This is kind of a long shot, but the homeowner association president is really looking for volunteers to help serve on the board. Do you know Zelda Smith?"

Emily smiled. "Only a little."

"Ms. Smith has been dying for me to serve, but I just don't have the time to fit it in with my job being as busy as it is." I hesitated. "I don't think it would be much *fun*, but you mentioned you were looking for something to do."

"You're such a sweet girl. Actually, that's exactly the sort of thing I should be doing. I guess Zelda just gave up asking me after so many years. But now I really *do* need to do something like that. Thanks, Ann. I'll get in touch with her." Emily reached out and patted my arm.

I said, "On a totally different subject, may I distract you for just a few minutes? You haven't met our latest librarian here."

"Oh, the new children's librarian? I saw her briefly when I first came in." From Emily's expression, I could tell she didn't have a wonderful first impression.

"Luna? She's great. And I'll introduce you to her, too. But I meant our feline visitor . . . as yet unnamed. Maybe you can enter our contest, too." I handed her one of the flyers from a nearby table. "Actually, a lot of people have been entering our contest already today. But I'm hoping for some better ideas." I noticed the stack of papers on the circulation desk where our patrons had been returning their votes had gotten larger since the last time I checked.

Emily's eyes opened wide. Apparently, I had pegged her correctly as a cat person. "A cat? Here? In the library? How wonderful!"

"He's a beautiful orange cat. From what I've heard, he was one of Elsie Brennon's cats."

"Oh, the poor woman. I was so sorry to hear about her car accident. And surprised! Elsie always drove twenty miles an hour," said Emily sadly. "I'm sure she would be so happy to know her cats were all right. She set such store by them, you know. They were almost like children to her. She always showed me their pictures."

I asked, "Do you remember what the cats looked like?" I asked.

"An orange and white cat and a tabby," said Emily promptly. "But I couldn't tell you their names, for the life of me. It's a good thing you have a contest. Not that cats really respond to their names unless they feel like it."

"Those sound like the cats we rescued. The tabby has already tentatively been adopted. The orange cat had such a rough day yesterday that I've had him cooped up in the breakroom. The vet asked me to keep him quiet after he was fixed. But I'm thinking a change of pace might be good for him. Would you like to take a book or a magazine into the Whitby historical room? I don't think he's quite ready to be in the rest of the library today, but I'd like to see how he does with you in another room."

Emily beamed at her. "I'd love that."

When I joined Emily again in the small room lined with old pictures, letters, books, and other Whitby artifacts, she was sitting in a large armchair with a cooking magazine in front of her. Her eyes widened at the sight of the orange cat purring in my arms.

I set the furry boy down on the floor and he immediately put two paws tentatively on the seat of Emily's chair as if asking permission to jump up and join her. What cat ever does *that*? The cat my great-aunt had had years ago trod all over my laptop and me with no compunction whatsoever. In fact, he'd seemed to revel in my dismay when he'd typed all over whatever document I was working on.

Emily clucked at the cat and he gave an easy jump up, bumping his head on her hand and rubbing his cheek against her before quickly settling down on her lap with a contented purr. He was dozing soon after.

Emily looked at me. "I think he's ready for the general library population. Seriously, Ann—what a sweetheart he is."

The cat had so far won over everyone who saw him. "I may give that a go tomorrow. Today was supposed to be a quieter day for him, but I'm not sure he'd even be overwhelmed at all with a room full of people. When the library closes tonight, I'll let him explore the rest of the library while it's empty and I'm still here to supervise."

Emily said, "And you're still trying to figure out a name for him? With the contest?"

"Luna and I thought we'd review the entries later and see which one seems to be the best fit," I said. Although the contest appeared to be really good today for patron involvement and awareness of the cat, I felt like we needed to dignify the furry boy with a name as soon as possible. This wasn't a contest that I was willing to let go on for weeks. "Do you have an idea?"

Emily gently stroked the cat's orange fur, and he purred louder in his sleep. "It would be fun to give him a literary name, wouldn't it? If he's to be a library cat? I may have an unfair advantage over the other folks entering the contest because I got to meet him. But he seems to me like he'd be a great Fitzgerald. Like F. Scott, of *Gatsby* fame, of course. He likes the good life, I think."

I gave her a smile. "Honestly, I could see that. And he's definitely the cat version of a man of the world, too, considering he was plucked from a culvert."

"Fitz for short," Emily said, scratching the cat under his chin to another explosion of purrs.

"It's a good name," I admitted. "I'll jot it down and see how it compares to our other entries. Because it's open to all our patrons, including kids, we're sure to get our fair share of 'Fluffies'. Nothing against *Fluffy*, of course," I added, since who knew what Emily's various cats were named?

"He definitely likes the good life," Emily reiterated. "Look how contented he is. I don't think you're going to have a problem with him trying to get back outside the door."

"That was another of my concerns," I said. "The last thing I wanted was for us to embrace him as a library cat and then have him disappear the next time a patron walks in or out the door."

"I just don't see him being one to hover by the door looking for a chance to exit," she said.

"And you're our cat expert," I said with a grin. "Thanks, Emily."

"Thanks to *you*," she said. "This has made my day. I'll just sit in here for a while with my magazine."

"When you're ready to go, just text me and I'll slide him back in the breakroom," I said, jotting down my number.

Chapter Eight

The next hour was spent following up for a patron on a challenging reference question while being intermittently interrupted by problems with self-checkout, logging patrons onto the computers, and showing a new volunteer around the library. I also made some flyers about the upcoming self-defense class with the police chief and put another reminder about it on our social media feeds.

At that point, Emily was ready for the orange cat to return to the lounge. I picked up the languorous animal, still purring in his half-sleep, made my goodbyes to Emily, and put the cat safely back in the breakroom.

Luna entered the breakroom and stooped to see the orange cat who was already a happy puddle at the continued attention.

"Everything okay with the upset lady?" asked Luna, giving her a sideways look.

"All fine. She was Roger's aunt and the one who set up our date to begin with," I said. "She thought a lot of her nephew and was understandably upset. But our new cat really seemed to settle her down. He has a calming effect."

Luna nodded and walked over to the fridge, pulling out what appeared to be a fearsomely fibrous salad with the incongruous side of a packaged honeybun laden with white icing. "You know, I've taken a glance through our entries online and in the library. They're not looking too good."

I made a face. "I glanced at it a little while ago and it looked like there were a lot of entries."

"Yeah, but have you *seen* the entries?" Luna chuckled. "There's nothing that really screams 'library cat' yet."

"How bad could they be?" I asked.

"Although you very carefully noted the cat's gender, there still appears to be some confusion out there. We have a Tinkerbell and a Molly and a Bella so far. The others are aggressively generic: Tiger, Morris, Leo."

I made a face, which could have also been intended for the weedy salad she was now consuming. "No terrific literary options?"

"None that I saw. Unless you want to count Tinkerbell," said Luna.

I considered this. "Ordinarily, I'd say we hadn't given anyone enough time to enter a name. And it's usually good to stretch these things out for better engagement from our community. But the truth of the matter is that this guy deserves a name and probably needs to be already learning it. Emily, Roger's aunt, did give me one suggestion: Fitz, short for Fitzgerald."

Luna nodded, tilting her head and considering the cat. "You know, I can totally envision that for him. And I like it better than some male literary names I was mulling over: Hemingway, Tom Sawyer, Queequeg, or Kafka."

I resisted making another face at Queequeg and Kafka. "I did think Heathcliff might be cute, but the cartoon strip sort of took over that one, didn't it?"

Luna said, "That sounds like the best one so far."

"I'll run it by Wilson when I have a chance," I said. "Although I got the impression he didn't so much care what name we choose as long as it's soon." I glanced at my watch. Breaktime was over, but I realized Luna had been on her own most of her first day and that Wilson, although a good boss in many ways, probably hadn't thought to check in with her much. It was a tribute to Luna's aura of equanimity and confidence that I hadn't even realized this. "How is the first day going so far? What kind of impression do you have of the library?"

She grinned at me. "It's perfect, I promise. Really, I appreciate that you keep checking in, but you asked me earlier."

"Just wanting to make sure you still feel good about the library closer to the end of the day. I'd hate to have you scared off on day one."

"No worries! It feels homey and cozy and safe. It's the kind of place where families come every Saturday to check out books and magazines and music for their kids. The folks are nice, they're mostly courteous, and there are always people in here and things to do. What's not to like?" asked Luna.

I nodded, feeling a little relieved. After the chaos of the last few months following CeCe Appleberry's abrupt departure as children's librarian, it was good to have this immediate feeling from Luna that she'd found a good spot to stick around in.

I could definitely handle the children's section and the story-times, but I'm not going to say I was the best candidate or that the extra work wasn't tough to juggle.

"That's great, Luna. Please just grab me if you have any questions or problems. And now my breaktime is over, so I'd better run."

"Sounds good. And hey—I wanted to thank you again for taking over for me for storytime this morning. I'm really sorry I was late. I thought I'd work late tonight to try to make up for it," said Luna.

I shook my head. "There's no need to do that, Luna. Wilson sure doesn't expect it. And there won't be a lot of folks here on a Saturday night."

"I know, but I feel bad. On my first day, too! I have a container of antibacterial wipes in my car and I thought I'd go through and wipe down all the toys in the children's section. And maybe the board book covers, too. Who knows what kinds of germs might be lurking on that stuff?" she asked with a lop-sided grin.

"Seriously, Luna, you should probably go home to see about your mother," I said. "Don't worry about it."

"I've already checked in with her and she has a lady from church dropping by to bring her a meal and visit for a bit, so I'd only be in the way while they talk about knitting and quilting. No, I think it will be fun to do a little cleaning. There's something really satisfying about it. How about you? Got any plans for tonight?" asked Luna, temporarily abandoning her grotesque salad for the glazed honeybun.

"Just a meal with a friend of mine," I said.

Luna raised her eyebrows. "A date?"

I made a face. "I don't think there will be any dates for a while. No, this is just takeout with my old college professor. I want to hear how his discussion with Burton went."

After work, I picked up the food and headed over to Nathan's house, a one-story brick house with a beautiful yard. Although Nathan had retired, he definitely hadn't chosen to withdraw from the community. He took long walks with his adorable Yorkshire terrier, Mr. Henry, speaking with neighbors along the way, visited the library regularly and took the occasional class there, and was involved with his church.

He beamed at me when he opened the door, his white hair, as usual, slightly askew. There was a tiredness in his eyes today, though, which wasn't ordinarily there. The diminutive Mr. Henry peered around Nathan, barking bravely at me. "So good to see you, Ann! Where should we sit . . . inside, or outside?"

I knew his backyard was a mini nature preserve, so I immediately voted for outside. He took the bag of takeout from me, grabbed some bottled waters from his fridge, and led me and a happily trotting Mr. Henry to his back patio. We sat at a small table that looked out on flowering azalea bushes, miniature magnolias, and a collection of bird feeders. Mr. Henry gave me a doggy grin and gazed with interest at me with his bright button eyes.

While we ate, Nathan talked about what he'd been doing: the book club he'd joined that he was now leading, the puzzle books he'd been devouring since he'd discovered how much he enjoyed cryptograms, and the fact he'd made a lady friend in town at church and was enjoying getting acquainted with her.

He seemed determined not to mention Roger Walton or the chief of police while we were eating.

Once we'd eaten most of our food, Nathan said quietly, "Now I suppose I should tell you how my afternoon went." He hesitated and said, "First off, tell me how you ended up involved with Roger."

Chapter Nine

"I never even had the chance to meet Roger, actually. You see, I have a patron named Emily," I started out.

Nathan interjected, "An older lady? Emily Walton?"

I smiled at him. "That's right. I forget sometimes how many people you know in Whitby. You can put all this in context better than I could by trying to explain the backstory."

He sat back in his chair, forgetting the Chinese takeaway for a moment as he thought. "Nice lady. Something of a busybody. She and I were on a committee together at the Presbyterian Church . . . a history of the church for its sesquicentennial and bringing in all sorts of Whitby history, too, of course, since those things would have been intertwined. She wanted, I think, to be *helpful*, but she wasn't very."

"How did she try to help you?" I asked.

He returned to the carton of takeout and pushed his noodles and broccoli around a little with his plastic fork. "Oh, the usual way, of course, with the project we were working on. But more than that. We started talking about our retirements. Well, Emily hadn't actually been a professional, but she had her deceased husband's investments and is on a fixed income like I am.

She started talking about her brilliant nephew and how much he had helped her to grow her capital." His voice took on a distinctly bitter tone toward the end. Mr. Henry nuzzled his leg, and he reached down absentmindedly to pat him.

"Burton is an interesting fellow," he said absently.

"Yes, I thought so, too. I think he's going to fit in well here because he's trying so hard to get out in the community," I said.

Nathan gave a small smile. "Of course, I had absolutely no idea what he was doing here. It caused quite a commotion on my street. All the neighbors were gaping. Everyone could see he was heading straight for my door."

I chuckled. "That must have been embarrassing. I guess you could tell everyone it had to do with needing to get your license plate registration updated or something mundane like that."

"Are you kidding?" asked Nathan with a twinkle in his eye. "I've eaten all the extra attention up. I'm surprised we don't have a crowd at my door asking questions even now. And the older ladies around here thought it was all very gritty-sounding." But the tiredness I'd noticed in his eyes were now etched around his mouth. He was more worried than he'd let on.

I raised my eyebrows. "That you were being questioned as part of a murder investigation?"

"Exactly." But the word *murder* did make him solemn. "And I'm sorry you were questioned, as well. I'm imagining they'd want to make sure your relationship with Roger wasn't somehow part of his death."

"The thing was that I didn't even *have* a relationship with him. And the more I find out about Roger Walton, the happier I am the date didn't happen. But yes, the initial questions definitely had to ascertain that fact." I led him through my arrival at the house, my conversation with Burton, and the time I'd spent with Roger's sister.

When I'd finished, I tentatively asked, "What did Burton say? Did you get the feeling you might be a suspect?"

Nathan said dryly, "Oh, I very *much* got the feeling I might be a suspect. I guess the chief had been talking to other employees at the investment office. Apparently, more than one of them mentioned my name." He sighed.

"I'm delighted you didn't have to have that first date or any other contact with him, because I thought Roger was a thoroughly bad sort of guy. But you're so astute that you'd have figured that out right away after having wasted only part of an evening with the man," said Nathan.

"Could you walk me through what happened to you?" I asked. "I got a sort of general idea, but it would be helpful to get the whole picture."

He sighed and gazed blankly across the backyard. "Well, I had the recommendation from Roger's great aunt Emily. She's either quite the cheerleader for her family or else she's just naïve enough to think they're all terrific people and gifted in business."

I hid a smile. "But you mentioned that he'd successfully invested for her in the past."

He waved his hands in the air at this. "Who knows about that? Maybe he put her in something ridiculously safe, or a sure thing. I will say this—the guy was very confident and very persuasive. Looking back on it, I can't really believe I fell for it."

"You're not saying they were scams, though. The investments?" I took a bite from my egg roll.

He shook his head. "Oh, no, not in the literal sense. He wasn't putting my money in some kind of pyramid scheme or something. But it just wasn't the right fit for me—considering where I am financially with a fixed income. My age should have been a factor, too. And now that I think back on it, and on him, he seemed like a really slick kind of character. The kind of person I *wouldn't* trust and the type that I'd see through."

I finished off my fried rice and pushed it away from me. "I know what you mean. I'm not usually taken in by those types, either."

Nathan said, "I had students like that, you know. They'd try to work their charm-offensive on me at the end of the semester to see if I'd give them some sort of easy extra credit or curve their grade when they'd been goofing off the entire semester, or hadn't been showing up to class."

I smiled. I knew what Nathan's answer to *that* would have been.

He said, "It all made me realize there were probably elements going on in the background. Perhaps Roger was getting kickbacks from the groups he was putting my money in. Whatever it was, it wrecked my finances. I don't have that nest egg anymore." He leaned forward, putting his hand on the table earnestly. "I don't want to give the impression that I'm impoverished or anything. But it wouldn't be very convenient if I had some sort of health setback and needed to move to a retirement home."

He seemed like he wanted to collect himself a little as his temper heated up thinking about it all. I carefully collected the trash and put them into the takeout bags and threw it all away in his cheerful yellow kitchen while he calmed down.

When I came back moments later, he was his usual urbane, thoughtful self again with more of a filter between him and his experience. And with Mr. Henry sitting happily on his lap.

"So I lost money. A good deal of it. Bled it out and rather quickly. I went to visit him to see what could be done," said Nathan.

I nodded. "In terms of just trying to switch to a better investment or have a plan moving forward?"

"Both. I wasn't a business professor, after all. I don't think my English degrees were going to help me in this situation. And, at the time, I think I was fairly levelheaded about the whole financial disaster." Then he stopped, soberly appraising this statement and gave a short laugh. "All right, perhaps not. But it wasn't as if I was heading over to Roger Walton's investment office to have him executed, or even fired. I was simply angry, anxious, and wanted to give him a piece of my mind."

"And apparently you did so?" I asked.

He pushed away from the circular table we were sitting at and I followed him to some heavily cushioned rocking chairs that were a few feet away. They were a lot more comfortable. I remembered now that Nathan got stiff if he sat in one spot for too long.

"I did certainly give him a piece of my mind, and then some," he admitted. "The problem was that even though I set out merely to chastise him and then move on to shoring up other potential investments to make up for the losses, he just so smugly refused to take on any culpability in the matter."

I rocked gently in the rocker. I could almost see myself falling asleep in this thing. "I'm playing devil's advocate here . . ." I hesitated, trying to find the right words.

Nathan looked at me sideways. "I know what you're about to say, and you're right. An investment counselor isn't technically culpable at all for an investment's performance. And the investor should always realize there are no guarantees in investing, and the fact is, they might just as well lose their money as make any of it. But I think there were extenuating circumstances here. Roger failed to tell me exactly how risky the investment was, and didn't indicate it might be inappropriate for me and my station in life. To be fair, I didn't ask any questions, either. Pure greed moved me forward," he added dryly.

"You wanted a simple apology," I said.

"I *wanted* my money back, but that obviously wasn't in the cards. And I wanted an acknowledgment from Roger that he'd screwed up in pushing me into the fund. And perhaps a statement from him agreeing that playing the market was practically akin to buying a lottery ticket or gambling . . . that it could be extremely dangerous in terms of losing nest eggs." He sighed. "I might have been a little unreasonable."

"And did he offer any sort of apology? Express any regret at all? Solace?" I was beginning to like Roger less and less. Perhaps this episode was going to put me off dating for even longer than the last bad date I'd had, over a year ago.

"None. And his attitude was just so cocky. He could only shrug and say that was just the nature of investing. Plus, he was trying to hurry me out of there—get rid of me. I figured he had some sort of big investor coming in right after me; one with deeper pockets," said Nathan. He looked broodingly across the backyard as we rocked. "I talked to his boss and complained about him."

"Did that do any good?" I asked.

He shrugged. "I doubt it. They probably mentioned it to him, but might have been rolling their eyes about me at the time. And, on my end, the more I thought about it, the angrier I became."

I said, "But this was a little while back, wasn't it? I mean, the former employee who mentioned it isn't even working for the investment firm now. It wasn't as if it happened last week. Why would the police think you'd suddenly decide to murder your investment counselor over it now?"

He was quiet for a few seconds and then said with a sigh, "Because I recently blew up at him in public."

I made a face. "Ah. That makes sense then. And 'public' for the town of Whitby means *everyone* knows about it. I'm surprised it didn't make the front page of the newspaper."

He laughed. "Only because it was a big news day for the paper. They were covering the local fishing competition. I can't say I'm not ashamed of myself. I never remember having this much of a temper. The truth is, I'd spent much of the night before awake—worrying about money. That's such a horrible way to spend a whole night, if you've never done it, and I hope you haven't."

"So you were sleep-deprived when you saw Roger out and about?" I asked.

"Right. I was picking up lunch at the deli and he was in there. I snarled at him. Then I even gave him a little shove when he looked as if he might be laughing at me. Of course, it was during the busiest time of the day for the deli and everyone in there was watching us. That's probably why the chief is focusing on me. Not only did Roger's coworkers tell him I'd been upset about the bad investment, but the folks who work at the deli likely told him about my confrontation with Roger."

He looked worried and I'm sure I looked the same. This wasn't good. "Did the police ask you where you were last night?" I asked slowly.

"They wouldn't have been doing their jobs if they hadn't," he said in a light voice. "I don't have a wonderful alibi, unfortunately. I was out and about yesterday evening. I could have done it. I'm strong enough, although the police said it wouldn't have taken as much strength as you'd have thought."

The thought of the skewer made me shiver, and I nodded. "I don't think they'd have written you off as too weak to be able to commit the crime." We rocked for another few moments and I said, "Do you have any sort of idea who might have wanted to do Roger in?"

"Besides me?" he asked wryly. "I'm afraid not. The only person I knew with a connection to Roger was his great aunt, and she was singing his praises and finding him clients and blind dates! No, I didn't know Roger well, and was happy to keep it that way." He scratched Mr. Henry behind his ears. He gave me a sideways glance. "Now, Ann, I know you're not going to want to hear it. And I hate sounding like all those people trying to give you dating advice."

I sighed and shook my head. "I think I know what's coming."

Nathan said, "It's just that you've buried yourself in the library. It's not good for a young person like yourself. You're spending what little free time you have with old fogeys like me."

I said lightly, "And I wouldn't have it any other way."

His expression was serious as he said, "Ann, I'm just saying maybe you should stop running away. Try getting over this fear of intimacy. I'm not only talking about romantic relationship, either. Maybe make a friend—besides me."

I took a deep breath. The problem was that Nathan saw right through me and knew me too well. He knew I had a tough time getting close to people. And he knew the reason why.

He put his hands up. "And that's all I'm going to say. I know it's none of my business, but I care about you as if you were my own daughter. Now let's move on to something else. Why don't you tell me something good? What's going on at one of my favorite places in the world?"

I smiled at him, relieved at the change of subject. "The Whitby Library? There are all *sorts* of good things going on there. Let me tell you about a couple of upcoming programs I think you might want to be a fly on the wall for. But first . . . I should tell you the story of our new resident."

His white eyebrows sprung up as if they were on springs. "Resident? At the library?"

"Indeed. And his name, although it's still being determined, *might* be Fitz."

Chapter Ten

"Let's go with Fitz," said Wilson decisively the very next morning before the library opened. The library opened at noon on Sundays and there were already some folks gathering outside the door. The library director was glancing through the social media votes and the sheaf of votes with a pleased expression on his face. "Say, this was terrific for public engagement. I don't know when our social media accounts have been so busy."

"Fitz it is," I said. "I didn't see anything else that seemed to fit him so well. Besides, I ran it by my former English professor last night. If even *he* couldn't think of something better, we're in good shape."

Wilson and I both gazed at Fitz. He'd spent the entire evening loose in the library since he'd already demonstrated himself an expert at the litter box the day before. The custodian was able to fashion a cat door on our custodial closet and Fitz clearly had gotten the hang of it overnight. I'd come over to the library at eleven to make sure there hadn't been any Fitz-related damage I needed to know about. I found him asleep on a table against a displayed row of Rosamunde Pilcher books. There was no evidence of any claw-sharpening, 'accidents,' or destruction of any kind. I'd vacuumed thoroughly before my conversation with Wilson.

"Fitz seems like a laid-back guy," said Wilson. The cat opened one eye and surveyed Wilson solemnly before closing it again. He tilted his head to one side. "So . . . we'll keep him out in the library today. He knows where his litter is." He set his face grimly. "If there are any complaints, refer the patrons to me."

"I will scoop him up with me to the breakroom at lunch, too," I said. "Maybe it would be good for him to take a break from people at that point."

Although, to be sure, it didn't seem like a concern. Fitz's love for people was already well-documented.

Wilson turned a stern expression on Fitz. I knew Wilson well enough to know this was an expression of deep thought and of analyzing a particular situation. But if you didn't know him, it would look as if he was very annoyed about something. He finally said, "Now, the last thing we need is for this cat, once the public latches onto him, to have something to happen to him. He doesn't need to be dashing out into a busy parking lot. Heaven forbid he gets run over with a library full of loving patrons watching."

We surveyed Fitz again. He rolled over on his back and opened an eye again at Wilson.

"It doesn't seem likely," I said.

"By the way, how did things go with Luna yesterday?" asked Wilson.

I smiled at him. "She fit in perfectly. She didn't ask a lot of questions, she took initiative, she introduced herself to patrons.

And the kids all seemed to love her. I think they thought she was some sort of fairy with her colorful clothes and purple hair."

Wilson looked puffed up. He liked to hear when he'd done something well. "Yes. I rather thought she'd fit in well." He gave me a look out of the corner of his eye. "Appearances can be deceiving, you know. In a library, we know not to judge a book by its cover."

"I know what you mean. I'll confess I wasn't really sure what to make of Luna at first. She does have a sort of big-city tough look about her, but Luna is about as tough as Fitz here," I said.

Wilson lifted his eyebrows. "Considering Fitz survived a flood in a gutter, I think that speaks to both his and Luna's levels of grit." He glanced at his watch. "The only thing I worry about is that she won't be *punctual.*"

I hid a smile. Wilson always reminded me of the White Rabbit from *Alice in Wonderland* when he started up with his punctuality rants. He'd stand there, looking at his large watch and worrying.

I said, "I know she's taking care of her mom right now and I have a feeling mornings are a rough time. Anyway, you know I'm always here at the crack of dawn to cover in case she's in five or ten minutes late."

Wilson batted his eyes a bit at the *ten minutes* part of that sentence, but seemed generally appeased.

Fortunately for Luna, she came in several minutes before the library opened to the public. What's more, she gave a rousing storytime that had the mothers applauding at the end of it. On the way out, she showed all the children how to rub Fitz gently if they wanted to meet him. Fitz had taken a lazy interest in the storytime and was curled up on a display we'd made of Junie B. Jones books. He gave little mews to the children and totally won them over.

A little later, I was at the research desk and one of our regular patrons came up to me with a look of concern. She was Sadie Stewart, a woman in her mid-thirties with brown hair and, lately, an exhausted expression on her face. She had her toddler with her, Lynn, who blinked sleepily at me.

"Everything okay?" I asked. It was a question that could lead to a patron asking about researching a particular health problem, or one that could lead to a patron reporting that the restrooms were out of order.

"That's what I wanted to ask *you*," she said. "I've heard about what happened with your date."

I looked ruefully at her. This was definitely something that came along with the territory of living in a small town. "I'm sure most of Whitby has, by now."

Sadie nodded and looked uncertain. "Sometimes the town knows things and sometimes not. I'm not sure if you knew I was in a relationship with Roger."

My mouth dropped open before I hastily snapped it shut again. "I didn't, I'm afraid. I'm so sorry! You were currently dating Roger when we had our date arranged? How awful." I glanced around to make sure there weren't a bunch of town residents horning in on our conversation, but everyone seemed otherwise engaged. That was good. The last thing I needed was for a rumor to start that I was some kind of homewrecker.

"No, no," she said hurriedly. "Roger had ended our relationship. I am not over here to give you a hard time or chastise you or anything. I felt bad that you had to go through finding him dead. And maybe I wanted to hear more about what happened."

I asked, "Roger had *just* ended your relationship?"

Sadie shook her head. "No. And, actually, it had been on-again-off-again for a long while. And maybe I hadn't *accepted* the relationship was over. He and I had history together, not all of it good. But it was good enough on the whole that I thought it would be worthwhile trying to make something of it."

She carefully set her toddler on the desk so she could reach for Fitz, who was sprawled out taking a nap. I made sure the toddler wasn't too grabby, but she seemed gentle and Fitz seemed happy.

"I'm so sorry," I repeated. "I'd never have agreed to go out with Roger if I'd thought he was in any sort of relationship. You see, I didn't even know him. One of his relatives set us up on a blind date."

As we watched her toddler, it occurred to me she could be Roger's child. Sadie caught me studying her and smiled, "She favors him, doesn't she?"

"Honestly, I never even met him, so I couldn't say. She's Roger's daughter?" I asked. I was stumbling now, really knocked off-guard. For some reason, I'd apparently assumed Roger didn't really have any kind of romantic backstory. Maybe it was just convenient for me to think he had a blank slate when it came to dating. But here was a woman I'd been acquainted with for years who'd had what was clearly a very intimate relationship with Roger.

"Roger wasn't the best at dealing with responsibilities. Maybe he was just in denial. Oh, I guess he helped me out from time to time. But I wanted more involvement. I wanted more *support*," she said, giving a short laugh. "Not just money. I wanted emotional support, too. And support from another parent. It's tough to be a single mom and sometimes I don't feel like I'm doing a very good job," said Sadie, looking tired. "Although my mom does help me a ton. I don't know what I'd do without her."

"You're doing a *great* job," I said firmly. "I know you work so hard with your daughter. You're checking out bedtime stories, you're checking out music for her to listen to. You're going to storytimes. Everything you do is designed to enrich your child."

Sadie brightened at this. "Thanks. Sometimes it's easy to lose perspective. I'll see what other parents are doing and I know I'm working with a really cramped budget and can't do all of the special, extra activities that other parents are doing. Thanks for making me feel like I'm doing all right."

I said slowly, "And you said you wanted to know more about my discovery of Roger." I briefly and as non-dramatically as possible filled her in.

Sadie listened closely and then was silent for a few moments. "That must have been awful. But it sounds like he didn't suffer. Was that your impression?"

I said, "I don't think he possibly could have. And maybe he wasn't even aware it was coming—he could have been caught totally off-guard by whoever did it. He would have been focused on getting the grill ready."

Sadie said slowly, "So the police are thinking it was someone he knew?"

I nodded. "For one thing, a stranger crime is really unlikely in Whitby. *Strangers* are unlikely in Whitby. To have some sort of itinerant killer coming through is not a scenario they're likely to pursue."

Sadie cleared her throat. "For the record, I was picking up Lynn at daycare when that was going on. Not that I'd have wanted to kill Roger anyway, despite all the trouble he's caused me. Although I sure have an idea who might have wanted to do him in."

I just waited, hoping Sadie would continue.

Fortunately, she did. "I'd put Heather at the top of the list."

I waited a moment for Sadie to explain why Roger's sister would have wanted to kill him. We watched as little Lynn laughed when Fitz reached out and touched her hand with a paw.

Sadie sighed. "I know I shouldn't gossip, but Heather and Roger didn't have the closest of relationships. Heather spent most of her time being mad at Roger."

"Why?" I asked, although I had the feeling it had something to do with their mom.

"For not doing what he was supposed to do. For not helping out." Sadie gave a short laugh. "I guess I didn't see it at the time, but Heather and I had exactly the same issues with Roger. We were upset he didn't take any responsibility for his family. And not only did he not help out financially or help spend time with his mother, but he also would tell Heather he was going to sit with their mom for a while for her to run errands—and then he wouldn't show up. That happened a lot," said Sadie. She made a face. "You must be hearing this and wonder why on earth I wanted to get back with him. I know I'm making Roger sound like he was totally unreliable, and I guess he was. But when we were together, we really had something special. And he wasn't always completely thoughtless. He could make incredibly romantic gestures."

And that apparently was the problem with Roger. He had been the kind of guy who was good at the gesture and bad at the everyday commitment.

Sadie glanced at her watch. "I should probably go. Thanks for talking to me—you've made me feel better that at least Roger didn't suffer at the end." She gently picked Lynn up and said, "I love the cat! What's his name?"

"We've decided on Fitz. Short for Fitzgerald," I said.

Sadie grinned at me. "A great cat deserves a great name."

The day grew really busy after that. Busy enough that it went in a blur and I didn't even realize it was time for a break until several minutes in. I hurried off to the breakroom to eat a few almonds I'd brought in as an energy-booster.

When I opened the door, I froze. Luna was crying, her head buried in Fitz's fur.

She jerked her head up and quickly wiped her eyes with her sleeve. I grabbed a few tissues from the box across the room and handed them to her.

"Thanks," she said, her voice muffled.

I walked over to get my almonds out, trying to give her time to compose herself—or to let her cry more, if she needed to. I was just thinking maybe I should take my snack back out to the circulation desk when she said, "Hey, sorry about this, Ann. You must think I'm a total mess."

I shook my head. "No way. You're just under a lot of stress right now. You've just moved back to a town you haven't seen for . . . what? Twenty years or so?"

Luna nodded ruefully.

I kept enumerating. "You're living with your mom. And taking care of your mom. And starting a new job. That's a lot going on at one time, Luna. And yet, since I've met you, you've been really upbeat and have kept a smile on your face the whole time. You're not a mess at all."

Luna gave me a grateful smile and then blew her nose with gusto. "Thank you. It's been a lot harder than I thought it would be. Usually, I can just handle stuff with no problems. I've always had a kind of happy-go-lucky personality. But this? This has been tough." She hesitated. "I think, on top of my mom's physical injuries, that she's a little depressed. This all started when she had knee replacement surgery. She asked me to move back home. I was surprised, but what could I say? Ever since her surgery, she really hasn't been the same. I was glad when her friend came over last night, like I mentioned."

"How did that go?" I asked.

She shrugged. "It seemed like it was okay. They were still visiting by the time I got home and Mom seemed like her old self—cheerful, fun. But then just half an hour after the friend left, Mom sort of deflated somehow. Half the time I'm trying to get her to do her PT exercises and the other half of the time I'm trying to persuade her to get out of the bed and get dressed. Part of me thinks I should stay at home with her, but it doesn't seem to make her any better when I do, plus we need the income from me working." She shrugged again and then chuckled. "I guess when I'm not sure what to do, the answer is 'cry'."

I said slowly, "I don't really know your mom, Luna. Maybe I've met her, but it's been a while since I did. Do you think she'd like to spend part of her day at the library? You could check in on her regularly. Do you think being around other people might do her some good?"

Luna considered this. "I'm not sure if she'd leave the house, to be honest. I've tried to get her to go out to supper with me, but she just doesn't want to. I guess I could give it a go, at least."

"The thing is, she could be totally quiet and by herself and still be surrounded by other people," I said. "You could pick her up or drop her off at lunch, if she needs you to drive her. I've got a film club meeting that's coming up . . . maybe she'd even enjoy it]."

Luna dabbed at her eyes again, a hopeful expression on her features. "Maybe. Maybe she'd go for that. I know she likes old movies. Thanks, Ann."

And suddenly, just like that, the conversation was over and she moved on to another topic.

"Hey, I tried the place you'd recommended yesterday. The vegan place a couple of blocks away. They had this amazing avocado and maple glazed tempeh sandwich that I think changed my life. At any rate, it cleared my head a little bit. As a bonus, I think I actually have a clue for you," said Luna, grinning at me. "I know you're trying to clear your professor friend."

"A clue? From the vegan deli?"

"From earlier. But first off, I'm wondering if you could show me a picture of Roger," said Luna.

Chapter Eleven

Although I didn't have a picture of my own, Roger was definitely on Google, considering the investment firm had all their counselors up on social media. I handed her my phone with the picture.

She studied it with narrowed eyes and then nodded. "Yep. That's him."

"You knew him? Or had met him?" I asked.

"Neither one. But I sure did hear him having a humdinger of an argument with someone not long before he croaked," said Luna in a level tone.

I felt my eyebrows fly up. "Really? Where was this?"

"Oh, I was grabbing lunch at a deli—different deli from today. The funny thing was it was sort of ironic because I'd just been reflecting on what a nice, quiet day I was having and what a very quiet town Whitby was. The next thing I know, I'm hearing this argument in hissed voices," said Luna.

"Who was the other person? Did you know him?" I asked.

"My answer would usually be no, since I'm so new here. But this guy I *did* know—he's my mom's doctor. Or *one* of her doctors, at any rate. His name is Kenneth Driscoll," said Luna. "In his forties, kind of handsome in a sort of Television Doctor way. And seems to think a lot of himself."

I nodded. "I know exactly who you're talking about. Everyone considers him to be the best family doctor in town."

"Well, that's a relief, since my mom really does need some good help and I'd have hated to make her change doctors, since she likes him so much. Although, I thought the guy acted like he was pretty big on himself. I think she likes him because he's tall, dark, and handsome," said Luna. Then she shrugged. "I dunno. Maybe I'm being uncharitable. He has a good way with Mom, and that's not always the case with doctors."

"So you saw them, what, waiting in line and having an argument?" I asked.

"No, that's the funny thing. It looked like they were sharing a meal together and I wouldn't have necessarily put those two together as friends, considering what you've told me about Roger and what I've seen of the good doctor," said Luna.

I thought about this for a minute. "Maybe Roger was advising him on investments? Maybe Roger gave him bad advice, too, like he gave my college professor."

Luna said, "Who knows? I'm sure the doctor probably has money to invest. I wish I could have heard more of what he was saying. All I know is it *definitely* seemed to be about money. At one point the hissing voice became louder and *money* was the one word I could make out."

I pulled up the library calendar on the computer and took a quick look. Then I smiled. "I thought I remembered correctly. It just so happens that Doctor Kenneth Driscoll is part of the Whitby Library's Health Awareness Fair tomorrow."

"Excellent!" said Luna. "You've got the perfect opportunity to talk to him. All I know is those two guys were *angry*. Considering one of them is dead now, it makes sense to follow up on it. Maybe it'll be a chance for the police to focus on somebody else."

I peered more closely at the calendar. "The self-defense class is also tomorrow at five. Let me check signups. I hate to have the chief give the class and not really have anyone to show up." I checked online and smiled. "Oh good. Looks like we have ten women. And I'm going to attend, myself." It looked like my little social media posts with Fitz had generated the interest in the program that I'd hoped.

"I'll do it, too," said Luna. "Since I'm off at five tomorrow. And that will give you a chance to catch Burton up to speed on all your investigating."

I gave her a wry look. "I'm sure he'll be delighted." I figured he might be more delighted that Luna was in attendance. Although, maybe I'd read that all wrong and he actually was fascinated by her for different reasons.

"Maybe he will. He's probably feeling a lot of pressure to make an arrest. I'd guess he needs all the help he can find."

I left for my lunch break not at all sure Burton would see things the same way.

After coming back from lunch, I spent time shelving books that had been returned to the drop box. I was putting away a slew of graphic novels when I heard a voice behind me calling my name.

I turned and smiled at Trista Terry. We'd been friends in college but hadn't seen each other in a while since both of us were busy with our jobs.

"Good to see you, Trista," I said.

She gave me a spontaneous hug. "Good to see *you*. Wow, it's been ages. We really need to catch up soon. Maybe we can grab a coffee or a drink sometime."

"That would be great," I said politely. I did want to hear how Trista was doing, but it pained me to admit Nathan was right—I wasn't exactly trying to make friends. I tried again and put a little more enthusiasm in my voice. "Just let me know what your schedule looks like. I'd love to hear what you're up to."

Trista made a face. "Oh, my life is all kinds of crazy right now. But I should be able to arrange something in the next couple of weeks. There *is* one thing that's going right—I *might* have a new relationship." She clamped her hands to her mouth in mock fear. "I better not say anything else or I might jinx it. By the way," she added archly, "I have an idea for a date for you. I'd love to set you up with this guy. I think you have a lot in common."

I made a face and said, "Please, no. I've had a few lately that haven't worked out exactly the way I wanted."

A flash of concern swept over Trista's face before it was quickly concealed. The problem with old friends is they know a little too much about you. I'm sure it was on the tip of Trista's tongue to ask me if I've dated anyone since Robert. Since college. But she was too polite to ask.

"Okay, then. I'll just plan on calling you in the next couple of weeks. Or maybe I'll see you when I'm back returning my book," she said brightly.

"What did you get?" I asked.

"*The Goldfinch*. I can't believe I haven't read it yet—I've heard so many good things about it. I'd better run . . . I'll see you soon, Ann."

The rest of the afternoon flew by and I was surprised to see it was six and time for me to leave for the evening since I didn't have to close up.

I drove home, my mind still thinking about things at work and the things I'd learned about people who were involved in some way with Roger.

I was tired as I got out of my car and headed up my front walk, but looking at the English garden on the way to my front door gave me pause. It was intended to be a riotous display of color and eclectic plants and shrubs. It wasn't supposed to be *quite* as riotous as it was now. And I was very suspicious several of the things flowering in the garden right now were not planted there but were weeds trying to pass themselves off as flowers.

I changed clothes, grabbed my gardening gloves and a pair of pruners, and headed back out the front. This was hardly the most stimulating of work, so I went *back* inside to grab a pair of headphones. I pulled up an audiobook I'd borrowed from the library: Donna Tartt's *The Goldfinch*. The narration was very good and soon I was sucked into the story again. Maybe I was *too* sucked in. I pulled up a couple of things that I realized did not necessarily qualify as weeds. I decided to move on to dead-heading some of the old blossoms. That was more of a thought-less task I could do without really paying much attention.

Listening as intently as I was, I didn't hear anyone come up behind me. I didn't hear a greeting. That's why I jumped about a mile and hollered when I felt a light touch on my shoulder.

It was the intriguing neighbor from down the street. He said something, but I didn't hear it with my headphones on. I ripped them off, quickly, face flushed.

"I'm sorry," he repeated. "I didn't mean to scare you. I'm Grayson Phillips."

He held out a hand, but I looked down at my dirty hands and winced. "Sorry, I'm absolutely filthy." I *had* used garden gloves, but only for part of the time. The things were so un-wieldy they made pulling hard sometimes. And I'm impatient with being clumsy.

He said quickly, "Of course you are! Sorry, that was silly of me. You're gardening, after all."

I somehow couldn't seem to find my equilibrium around this man. The first time I'd seen him, I'd walked past him on a stroll and tripped up over a loose spot in the sidewalk, flailing wildly before somehow landing on my feet. He'd called out to me to make sure I was all right and I'd waved a thanks, not want-ing to prolong my embarrassment. And now I struggled to find words.

"That's right. It's a nice change after my day job," I finally said.

"Which, I gather, is an indoor job?" he asked with a smile.

I nodded. "At the library. It might involve papercuts, but no dirt." I frowned, remembering an incident last year. "At least, not usually." I paused. "I hear you have a pretty fabulous job."

"Do I?" he asked, frowning.

"At least, *I* think so," I said, aware I was blabbering, but unaware of how to stop it. "I absolutely love music. One of the nice things about being at the library is I know all of the things in our collection—including music. I like pretty much everything, don't you? I mean, I suppose you'd have to, being a DJ."

Grayson blinked at me. "I'm afraid I'm *not* a DJ, actually."

"No?" I asked. I thought very bad things about the henna-haired Zelda Smith. It was almost as if she'd purposely sabotaged me. I gritted my teeth.

"I'm afraid not," he said apologetically. He added hurriedly, "Although I do enjoy music, of all different genres. It's rare there's something I don't like."

I was smiling and nodding, but barely listening to a word he was saying.

He cleared his throat. "The reason I came by was about the homeowner association thing. Sorry, I just don't have anyone's phone number right now so it's easier to run by. Ms. . . . Smith, I think it is? She said you'd thought I might be interested in serving on the homeowner association board. But I just don't have the time right now. Maybe one day."

I felt a sinking sensation inside. "I suppose I suggested it." I sighed. "Honestly, I was just trying to save myself in the process. Sorry. I've thrown you under the bus. Zelda Smith has been determined to rope me in for ages and I'm just about run out of excuses. The only problem is my excuses are all true. I really just don't have time to do it. I'm usually at the library both early and late and on weekends." I skittered to a stop. The man hadn't come over to hear *my* excuses.

But he only grinned at me. "Sounds like we're in the same boat, then. I successfully avoided it this time, anyway."

I chuckled. "Just stay on your guard. She doesn't ever give up." I paused. "Although, we might be safe for a little while. I recommended the open position to a friend of mine. Fingers crossed she ends up taking it."

Grayson said, "I'll let you get back to your gardening. Sorry to have disturbed you."

I just smiled rather vacantly at him and then hurriedly busied myself with pulling up something I later discovered was most definitely *not* a weed.

The next day was a busy one. Some of our library programs did super well and others were more lightly attended. But the Health Awareness Fair was always a huge hit. That's because there were free blood pressure and blood sugar checks, body mass index, and cholesterol screenings. The medical staff that attended also advised on a variety of different conditions, as well as promoted generally healthy habits.

The community room was completely filled as well as much of the library. And then we had our normal patrons, too, on top of it all.

Luna walked up to me at one point. "It's crazy in here!"

"Fortunately, we don't host the event too often," I said with a chuckle.

"Seriously, I could use a drink," she said with a sigh.

"Beer?" I guessed.

She snorted. "More like a rosemarycano."

"I don't even know what that is," I said.

"You're missing out. Campari and vermouth Americano with rosemary." Luna saw my expression and laughed. "I'm full of surprises. I once had a wealthy boyfriend in New York. It was quite the education." A mom walked up to ask her a question, and she hurried off.

Halfway through the event, I spotted Kenneth Driscoll, our local doctor. I could see why Luna would think he was cocky. He had a sort of smug look about him and he was certainly handsome. But also very good at what he did, and I'd never heard anyone complain about him.

At one point, he walked up to the research desk where I was sitting. "I brought my lunch with me—is there anywhere I can take a quick break to eat it before finishing up at the fair?"

I stood up. "As a matter of fact, it's time for my own lunch break. If you'd like, you can join me in the librarian's lounge."

"Thanks," he said and followed me as I scanned us into the breakroom. I scanned Fitz in there, too, since he was trotting along behind me.

"Okay if the cat joins us?" I asked.

Kenneth glanced down, just noticing the orange cat. "Sure, I guess."

He sat down at the table and I warmed up the broccoli and cheese soup I'd brought for my lunch. I thought about ways to bring up Roger's death and couldn't think of a natural way of doing it. Maybe it would be best if I pretended I was the one who'd seen him arguing with Roger at the deli, since it would be weird to tell him someone I knew had mentioned it.

When I sat down to join him at the table, he was already halfway through a sandwich and was reading one of the magazines littering the breakroom tables and chairs.

I took a deep breath and plunged in. "This is going to sound a little abrupt, but I think I've seen you recently. It's just a little awkward because you were having an argument with someone I knew."

As I'd expected, Kenneth's head jerked up, and he stared at me, a defensive look in his eyes. "What is this?"

"It's just something I'm curious about. As a librarian, curiosity is sort of my superpower," I said with a smile, trying to ratchet down the tension a little.

Kenneth still looked suspicious. "A superpower or a fatal flaw. Why do you care about an argument? Not that I'm saying there was one," he quickly added.

"You *were* engaged in an argument at the deli with Roger Walton, right?" I took a sip of my soup and tried to look just mildly interested in his answer.

He sighed and rubbed his eyes with the heels of his hands. "Yeah. That's right. But I can promise you the only reason my temper got out of hand is because that guy let his temper get out of hand first." He paused and looked at me. "So what are you—his girlfriend or something?"

I shook my head. "I was supposed to have a blind date with him Friday night. The thing is, though, when I showed up for the date, I found Roger dead in his backyard."

Kenneth's eyes opened wide.

"So maybe you can forgive my nosiness in this particular instance." I gave the soup a stir since it had reheated unevenly in the microwave. The last bite had burned my tongue.

Kenneth was quiet for a moment as if collecting his thoughts. Then he said carefully, "As a physician in this town, you know I have a position to maintain."

I shrugged. "I'd think you'd have considered that position before engaging in a public argument with someone."

He sighed and then rubbed his eyes again. "You're absolutely right. And I can't blame you for wanting to ask questions. Of course, it must seem there could have been some sort of connection between me and Roger Walton. But I can promise you there wasn't."

"And you frequently have lunch with people you don't know?" I asked, a tinge of asperity creeping into my voice. I tried to make my face more neutral. For some reason, Kenneth Driscoll and his superior attitude got under my skin.

"I'm having lunch with *you* now," he said pointedly. Then he stopped himself. A moment later he continued in a calmer tone. "I'm not saying I didn't know Roger. But I only knew him on a professional basis, as a patient of mine. I went out for a quick lunch and happened to see him eating there. I sat down with him for a few minutes and that was it."

"What were you so angry about?" I asked.

A flicker of fury briefly showed in his eyes. "*He* was the one who was angry. Then I reacted to his anger. I admit I shouldn't have. I brought up his bill, that's all."

I lifted my eyebrows. "His bill? You're not exactly working in accounts receivable. Are you very conversant on who owes money to your practice and who doesn't?"

He shrugged. "It's a small town, and therefore a small business. Although I'm a physician there and have office staff, I know a lot more about what goes on in the business side than doctors in bigger cities. The staff had mentioned they had a tough time getting hold of Roger and of extracting any sort of payment from him for services rendered about a year ago."

"It must have been a significant amount of money for them to be concerned about it," I said.

Kenneth said, "I can't discuss patients or their treatments. But it was a procedure, yes. It wasn't just a regular office visit or something like that. As I mentioned, I happened to see him there, remembered there was a problem collecting payment, and sat down to discuss it with him. He became angry and defensive and I became angry in return. It annoyed me that I'd performed a service and Roger thought I didn't deserve compensation for it."

"And that was the only time you saw him outside the office?" I asked.

He gave me an amused look. "I hope you're not imagining I would murder Roger. That wouldn't be a very effective way to get my payment, would it?" He paused. "When did he pass away? I can probably tell you what I was doing at the time."

"Friday night."

Kenneth pressed his lips together in annoyance. "I was working late at the office. I had to catch up on some notes, answer some emails from patients, and do the other red tape doctors have to put up with these days."

"Can anyone in the office vouch for that?" I asked.

He shook his head as if in amazement at my impudence and gave a short laugh. "They'd all left for the day. Look, I'm sorry about what happened to Roger and I understand you want questions answered. But it had nothing to do with me. You need to be talking to somebody else. Not that I know who 'someone else' might be. I didn't really know the guy. And don't imagine I had a motive, either. I have plenty of patients who don't pay—some of them are here in the library right now. And you can see I haven't been trying to play debt collector. Instead, I've been helping by volunteering at an event that should help the community be healthier."

I could tell the PR side of him was cranking up and that I wouldn't get anything further. "Okay. Thanks for that, by the way. The event is a huge success. I bet you're catching all sorts of health issues and helping to prevent them from getting worse."

He gave me a more genuine smile. "Thanks. I hope so. Early detection is really key for most of the big stuff." He stood up. "I'd better get back to it."

Chapter Twelve

By the end of the afternoon, I was setting up the community room for the self-defense class by pulling chairs and tables into a roomy closet.

Wilson stuck his head in the door and held out an envelope. "Mail for you."

"Mail?" I asked. I smoothed down my hair absently, realizing it was sticking up in the back from the furniture moving. "When do I get mail at the library?"

I took it from Wilson and frowned. "This isn't even mail. No stamp. Looks like someone must have dropped it off."

He shrugged. "Well, they dropped it off in a pile of library mail. I know the best way to find out more—open it up."

I did and then stared at the single sheet of paper inside.

"What is it?" asked Wilson.

"It's a warning," I said slowly. I held up the paper so Wilson could see what I did: *Stop Being Snoopy*.

Wilson sputtered and then said, "And someone dropped this off for *you*? What does it even mean?"

"I think it means someone thinks I'm asking too many questions about Roger Walton's death," I said. I took a deep breath.

Wilson's eyebrows drew together to form a woolly line. "What's the event you're preparing for?"

"Chief Edison's self-defense class," I said. My voice sounded curiously toneless to my ears.

"Perfect," said Wilson crisply. "We'll hand this over to him right away then."

I said, "It looks like it was written on a computer and it's been stuck in a plain envelope. There's no handwriting. Probably no fingerprints. And there aren't even any threats listed. Like I said, it's more of a warning."

Wilson said, "I don't care what the thing says or what clues it does or doesn't provide. No one sends warnings, threats, or anything like them to my staff at this library." He glanced up and saw Burton Edison tapping at the glass door outside the room. "Excellent. Perfect timing."

Wilson handed the letter to Burton. "Here's something you need to see. It was apparently dropped off here."

Burton read it silently and then looked up at me. "Does this make sense to you?"

I felt myself flushing a little. Wilson said, "She's apparently been looking into things a little."

Burton raised his eyebrows. "Have you? Why?"

Wilson glanced out the glass door and said, "Excuse me; I need to help out front." He hurried out of the room.

I said slowly, "I've been worried about a friend of mine, for one. Nathan Richardson."

Burton raised his eyebrows. "The retired professor? He's a friend of yours?"

"He was my favorite professor in college and we've become good friends. I hoped maybe I could find out some information to put him in the clear—or maybe redirect your investigation," I said. I flushed. It sounded a little crazy when I said it. Absently, I fingered the locket I wore.

Burton tilted his head to one side, watching me. "I'm also remembering what you told me Friday night at Roger's house."

"What was that?" I asked, trying to think back over our conversation.

"Just your backstory—the fact you said you didn't feel the world was a safe place after your mom died. That must really have affected you. Being that little and losing your mom."

I sighed. "I wish I remembered more about my mom, but I was all of eight years old when I lost her. Mostly, I just remember the nightmares I used to have."

He nodded to the locket, which I hastily let go of. "Was that your mom's?"

"It was. I wear it every day," I said with a short laugh. "It's a way of remembering her, I guess.

"Still, it must have really impacted you. Must have made you want to be safe," said Burton.

I nodded. "Actually, you're right. Mama's death was . . . well, it wasn't natural. She was taken before her time. My mother was the victim of a random act of violence. Someone broke into our house one night. I was asleep—at least I was until I heard the gun go off. My aunt explained later that my mom had surprised the burglar. Then, when the police caught a suspect, I had to go into the station and identify him. I'd seen him when he was leaving." I shivered.

Burton blew out a deep breath. "That must have been awful. I can't imagine bringing an eight-year-old into the station to identify her mother's killer."

"The police did their best to assure me I would be fine—that the man wouldn't be able to hurt me. But I was always so scared he'd come after me later because I'd been the one who'd gotten him locked away."

Burton shook his head. "*He* was the one responsible for that. If he wasn't happy about going to jail, he shouldn't have committed a crime."

I said, "That's what my aunt told me, too. Maybe I was just too little to be rational. I had nightmares forever until I realized how quiet and secure Whitby seemed. It was the perfect place for a kid who wanted life to feel safe again."

Burton shrugged. "I'm no psychologist; I'm just a cop. But it seems to me you're probably more invested than most folks in making sure Whitby *stays* safe. Plus, you've made a self-defense class possible," he pointed out.

I smiled at him. "You must be a detective or something," I said lightly.

Burton said, "I'm starting to think you must *want* to be one. What have you found out?"

I told Burton about talking to Mary Hughes, Nathan, and Kenneth Driscoll. He listened carefully and made notes in the little notebook he kept in his shirt pocket.

When I'd finished, he said, "So, Dr. Driscoll. That's one on me. I'd heard from other people about Mary and Nathan and have spoken with them. But the good doctor is a new one for me. How did you find out about that?"

I said, "One of my coworkers overheard an argument between him and Roger. She told me about it."

He said, "Well, I thank you. You've not only given me some helpful information, but you've also provided very thoughtful impressions of the different people involved. You make a good resource."

I grinned at him. "So I'm not going to get warned off from asking a few questions?"

He looked down at the paper. "I think somebody's already taken care of that for me." He sighed. "I'll take this note with me, but you know we don't have a huge forensics department—actually, we don't have a forensics department at all. Besides, although this was clearly a warning, there's no specific threat for me to act on. It was written on regular computer paper from a regular word processing program. And the person, if they had any brains at all, would have used gloves."

"I'm not really worried about it," I said. "I think somebody just got worried I'm getting too close."

"*I'm* a little worried you're getting too close," he said.

"Then the fact I'm about to take a self-defense class led by the chief of police is a matter of good timing," I said with a smile.

He chuckled. "That it is." He paused for a moment and then said, "So who do you think might have been upset with your questions? Who seems most likely? And what do you think you've found out that makes someone feel threatened?"

I considered this and then admitted, "I can tell you who gave me the most pushback, and that was Doctor Kenneth Driscoll."

Burton raised his eyebrows. "Is that so?"

I said quickly, "I'm not saying he's responsible for Roger's death. But he was very defensive, and he seems to be extremely protective over his reputation in the town."

"Understandably. Who wants to visit a physician who might be a killer?" said Burton dryly.

"I'll admit I can't somehow see him sending me anonymous notes, but maybe that's the point. Maybe receiving an anonymous note is meant to steer me in another direction," I said.

Burton nodded. "Could be. Hard to say at this point. Look, you're getting some good information, but I don't need another dead body on my hands—got it?"

"Of course," I said quickly. But in my head, I was already considering what my next move might be.

Burton asked, "On another topic, was there interest in the self-defense class, or is it going to just be you and me?"

"Actually, there was a good deal of interest, considering the short notice we gave everyone. Including me, there are twelve now," I answered.

Burton asked in a carefully casual voice, "Is your colleague going to be there?"

"My . . . you mean Wilson?" I asked. Part of me realized he *must* mean Luna, but the word *colleague* threw me off. If you looked the word up in the dictionary, it most certainly would not have a photo of Luna next to it.

Burton shook his head. "No, I mean your new coworker. I can't remember her name."

This from a man who gave every indication at having an excellent memory and being very good with name retention. "Luna. Luna Macon," I said. "And yes, she's planning on making it. She's our twelfth, actually."

Burton nodded, but I could tell he was pleased before he turned away. "Good," he said gruffly. "After all, you two are frequently leaving here at night. Parking lots are scary places. It's always good to keep an eye out." He paused. "And I didn't bring this up before, but you really should have made your blind date at a more neutral location. A coffeehouse or a restaurant or something."

I gave him a wry smile. "You're so right. I thought the same thing when I was standing at his front door and ringing the doorbell. Just because someone's great-aunt Emily thinks he's great doesn't mean he's not trouble. And I'm always so cautious and safety-conscious! I'll be more careful in the future—promise." Not that I was planning on going on any more blind dates in the near future . . . if ever.

The self-defense class went really well. I was, again, surprised by Burton and his friendly and matter-of-fact ease with everyone who attended. He displayed a great sense of humor, which helped with making the students feel relaxed. Luna exchanged banter with him, which also broke any ice that was present. I wondered if Luna was even aware of the number of times Burton's gaze shifted her way. Maybe she was used to people staring, considering her rather colorful appearance.

Despite the levity, Burton became deadly serious when showing the techniques, which he made us all repeat until we felt comfortable with them and displayed some skill at them.

I felt bad about how much time Burton was taking with this. He must have been tired after a long day of investigating

Roger's death. I appreciated that Burton wanted everyone to nail the self-defense techniques, but we ended up the class about two hours later. Then I spent the next couple of hours getting organized for the next day and helping a patron with a computer issue.

When I got home that night, I wasted little time relaxing since I was so worn out. The note, which I'd made light of with Wilson and Burton, seemed more ominous in the quiet of my house. I narrowed my eyes angrily. My home was my sanctuary, just as the library was. I wasn't going to let that be taken away from me by some ridiculous anonymous note dropped off by somebody too cowardly to sign a name. Just the same, I took special care making sure the doors were locked and the curtains drawn.

I fell into bed that night, completely exhausted. But hours later, I woke with a start, shivering. Nightmares. I hadn't had those in years.

The next morning, I headed out early to the library again, thinking I'd knock some work out before we opened to the public. I decided to grab a bagel for breakfast at a shop that wasn't far from the library.

But when I pulled up to the shopping center, I saw flashing blue lights in front of the tanning salon. At first, I thought maybe Burton had pulled somebody over or maybe there had been some sort of fender bender in the parking lot. But then I noticed nobody was in the parking lot at all—it seemed that it had to do with something inside the tanning salon.

I hesitated and then drove closer to the salon. I got out of my car. I could see an employee, one who definitely wasn't Mary, and Burton. Burton, face set grimly, escorted the employee out of the salon. He motioned for her to stand away from the building. She was a young woman and was crying, face flushed.

Burton caught sight of me and held up a finger to indicate for me to wait a minute. I saw him talking on his radio and then he motioned for me to come forward. The employee watched as I walked over to speak with Burton.

"It's Mary Hughes," he said. "Her coworker found her dead this morning."

Chapter Thirteen

"**D**ead?" I asked, gasping. "What, like natural causes?"

"She's been murdered," said Burton. "I have the state police coming over now. If you'll excuse me?"

The salon employee, still tearful, had apparently been told to wait outside, too. Burton started securing the scene. The employee walked over to join me, apparently not wanting to be by herself. She, like Mary, had a golden tan. But, despite the tan, I could see she looked pale at her discovery.

"Do you know Mary?" she asked, her face wet with tears.

I shook my head. "Not really. As I matter of fact, I only just met her. Can you tell me what happened in there? The police chief told me Mary had been murdered?"

This threatened to make the employee start crying again, but she took a deep breath and nodded. "I guess so. I mean, yeah, there's no other way she could have gotten hurt. Somebody did that to her."

"Did what?" I asked.

The employee took another shaky breath. "Hit her over the head. It was with that heavy doorstop we always use on nice days to prop the door open. Sometimes we get foot traffic from other stores that way. Or, at least, people coming in to hear our prices and specials."

"I'm so sorry," I said. "It must have been such a shock to find her."

The employee looked blankly toward the salon. "Mary didn't really even want the morning shift today, but I had a doctor appointment scheduled. At the last minute, the doctor's office called and said he'd been held up in surgery and would need to reschedule me. So I called the salon to tell Mary I could switch back out with her."

I nodded. "Did she answer the phone?"

The girl shook her head. "Nope. And that wasn't like Mary at all. Mary's the kind of person who's really *on* it. If she's working, she's working. She's not messing around like some people. So, I thought that was weird. I mean, even if she was talking to a customer, she'd take a quick call, even if it meant putting the caller on hold. Then I tried her cell phone and she didn't pick that up, either."

"So you drove over to see for yourself?" I asked. "You must really have been worried."

"It was just totally out of character for Mary. Yeah, I was worried. I didn't think something like *this* had happened, but I wondered if maybe she'd had a heart attack or a stroke or something like that. I don't think she was in the very best of health or anything. When I got here, the door was unlocked and there wasn't any sign of her." The girl swallowed hard.

I winced because I had the feeling I knew where the girl had found her. "And you looked for her."

"Right. Because it didn't make any sense. Mary wouldn't leave the salon with the door unlocked. And she always answered her phone, like I said. Then I found her in one of the tanning beds." She gave a shuddering sigh.

"And you said she'd been hit with the doorstop?" I asked.

She nodded. "I guess whoever did it walked back there and hit her over the head with the doorstop while Mary was checking the tanning beds first thing. Then I guess they shoved her in one so no one could see her from the door . . . maybe to give them some extra time? Anyway, the doorstop was still there on the floor next to the tanning bed."

The girl gave a short laugh. "You know, I didn't even really *like* Mary all that much. But I'd never have wanted something like this to happen to her. And I can't imagine who'd do something like this. Mary isn't married. Honestly, she can be difficult to get along with and I think that's why she's single. I barely knew her since she was a new employee, but the salon owner had us both working on the weekends for a while. She thought it would be busy then, but it was totally dead and so Mary and I had lots of time to talk. She mentioned she was married when she was very young and right out of school, but it didn't last longer than six months. And she told me her parents were deceased and she wasn't close to any of her other relatives. So I don't know if this is some kind of crazy, random crime or what."

I paused. "I'm going off the assumption this wasn't a robbery and that it was personal, but maybe that wasn't the case. Was there anything valuable in the salon?"

The girl said quickly, "Oh, there's nothing missing. We wouldn't have had any cash on the premises. Most of our customers are regulars and we draft their bank accounts or they pay with a debit card. Any cash in the store goes right to the bank right after we close every night. And unless someone can drag out a four-hundred-pound tanning bed, there's nothing to steal in there except an outdated computer."

"So it must have been a personal motive," I said.

The girl shrugged. "Like I said, I didn't really know her. But I do know she liked to gossip. Sometimes it seemed like Mary knew everything about everybody. I made sure I didn't share any secrets with her, let's put it that way. Maybe someone didn't really like that."

I said, "How has Mary been acting lately? Has she been her usual self, or a little different?"

Fortunately, the girl didn't seem to mind the questions. In fact, her tone was gossipy, too. Maybe Mary *was* a gossip, but it sure seemed like her coworker was, too.

The girl said, "She's really been stressed out lately, which is probably why she was such a pill to work with. I know a couple of times at work she got calls on her cell phone from debt collectors."

I said thoughtfully, "Maybe she hadn't cut back on expenses or her lifestyle after leaving her last job."

"Yeah. She always bragged about her old job, which was annoying. I'm like, 'if it was so great, why did you leave?'" The girl rolled her eyes.

"Did she say why she left?" I asked.

She shook her head. "Nope. But it sure wasn't to make more money by working in a tanning salon."

I remembered Mary had said her coworker had told her about Roger's death. I said slowly, "I did have a conversation with Mary recently. She mentioned you'd told her about Roger Walton's death."

The girl looked blankly at me. "Who?"

"He was Mary's coworker at her old office."

The girl shook her head. "Sorry, I don't know anything about that."

Burton came back out of the building and motioned to the girl.

"Better go," she muttered.

I figured the same thing. Instead of getting to the library early, I was going to be there right on time—if I hustled.

A couple of hours into work, I moved to the community room to host one of our book clubs. This one I particularly liked. It had a wide range of people in it—men and women, younger patrons and elderly. It made for interesting conversation and book discussions. Plus, Sadie's mother was almost always there. I wondered if maybe her mom might have any thoughts about Sadie's relationship (or lack of one) with Roger.

This time both Sadie's mother *and* Sadie were there. Sadie had her toddler, Lynn, with her and wasn't participating in the book club meeting, but she'd driven her mother there. This Tuesday book club was in the late morning. There were a few patrons who came during their lunch hour, but it was mostly retirees.

Sadie's mom, Louise, was a retired teacher in her mid-sixties. She always wore colorful slacks and tops and a cheery scarf. She smiled at me as she entered the community room. Louise was the first one there, as usual.

"You're here nice and early," I said, smiling back at her.

"I'm excited about talking about the book," she said. "I'd always heard good things about *Pride and Prejudice*, but I'd never actually read it. It wasn't a popular book to teach when I was in school. Besides, Sadie could bring me here early today, so I took advantage of it." She leaned in and whispered, "Bless her heart, she's a horrible driver. I'm always clutching the door in fear of my life. But I'm so grateful she drives me around. My driving days are through as of a couple of weeks ago. I suppose I wasn't such a wonderful driver, myself."

"How is Sadie doing?" I asked politely. Naturally, I also had other motives for asking this question.

Louise sighed. "She is just totally overloaded, but thanks for asking. The poor thing. Her days are crazy. She drops Lynn off at daycare and then is running right off to work."

"Where does she work again?" I asked.

"Sadie works over at the gym. She checks people in, makes sure the equipment is working, and even teaches a couple of the classes." Louise shook her head. "It's not a bad job, but she comes back home exhausted and sometimes she works really weird hours—later at night, very early in the morning, weekends, holidays. And I think working with the public and all the long hours really exhausts a person. Well, you'd know about working with the public!"

I smiled at her even though I found working with the public rather invigorating—most days. You never knew what people were going to do or say next and that's what made the days so interesting. There was nothing repetitive about working at a library and there was always the element of surprise. The surprise could be anything from a no-show from the teacher of the library's computer basics course to a patron who sheepishly realizes the book they heatedly insisted they'd returned to the library was actually in the back seat of their car.

Louise continued, "Then Sadie picks up Lynn at preschool and cooks supper. Half the time she cooks enough supper for me to have some too. Since I'm not driving, she and Lynn will pick me up and bring me to her house. We'll eat, sometimes I'll help read Lynn a story or help with her bath, and then Sadie drives me back home. She has a very busy life. But she wouldn't have it any other way. That's how it *should* be, though. We Stewart women would do anything for our babies."

Her fierceness reminded me of my aunt, who would also have done anything for me. She effectively had her entire life turned upside-down when I came to live with her, but handled it beautifully. Not only had she given me the safety I was looking for, but she had made life *fun* again. She'd also encouraged me to step out of my shell as much as I could. Just the same, I wasn't sure I was up to having a family of my own. I wasn't sure I could live up to becoming the role model my aunt had been.

"That does sound really hectic," I said.

"Plus, she has all of those medical bills. I know those keep her up at night. I don't think she sleeps half the time, and that's not good for her," said Louise.

"Medical bills? I'm sorry, I didn't realize she'd been ill," I said.

"Oh, they weren't for her—they were for Lynn. She had this terrible stomach bug a few months ago and the poor little thing became dehydrated. She spent several days in the hospital and Sadie was right by her side, of course. I don't have a lot of money, but I've always tried to help pay for some extras for Lynn—a preschool art class, a few toys, that kind of thing. But I couldn't even be of much help with those bills. They've been horrible, and they kept coming in the mail for longer than we thought. Really, she's still getting bills months later. Sadie has been really struggling to keep up. She's been so incredibly stressed. Every time I look at her, I see how exhausted and anxious she seems." Louise paused and then laughed. "Sorry, I shouldn't be unloading this on you. I sound like one of the Bennets from *Pride and Prejudice*, don't I? If only there was a Mr. Darcy out there for Sadie."

I said, "Is she in a relationship now?"

Louise laughed again, but this time it was harder. "No. She hasn't had the time or the energy. Although I'd babysit for her, of course, if she had a date. Lynn's a good girl and I love keeping her. But Sadie was really burned the last time she had a boyfriend. Roger."

I said, "Roger Walton, right?"

Louise nodded. "Of course I feel bad such a young man would pass away. But I can't say I'm grieving for him. He could be very unpleasant, and he didn't help with Lynn whatsoever. Sadie could really have used the financial support. And she hated the idea that Lynn was going to grow up without really having a relationship with her father."

I said, "That's a shame. Roger was her dad, after all. You'd think he'd have *wanted* a relationship with Lynn. Would have treasured it."

"He was only her dad in the technical sense of the word. He didn't do a blessed thing to help Sadie out. He could have seen the child on the weekends or taken her to a doctor appointment. Even if he didn't want any personal involvement, he could still have helped pay a hospital bill or even Sadie's power bill. He didn't want anything to do with either of them," said Louise.

I frowned. "But surely he must have had some sort of legal obligations to help provide support for Lynn."

"By the time Lynn was born, their relationship was over. As a matter of fact, it was over when Roger found out Sadie was pregnant. That's the kind of man he was," said Louise, her voice trembling a bit with anger. "Sadie didn't even list him on the birth certificate. And to force him to help her financially would have meant a lawyer and court dates—she certainly couldn't afford that, and he knew it."

I absorbed this for a second. Again, the more I heard about Roger Walton, the less I liked him.

The door opened and several of our book club members came in, one of them calling out a greeting to Louise, who waved back at them. "Thanks for letting me unload like that. I think the gist of what I was trying to say was Sadie is such a *good* girl. With all she has going on in her life and with as little help as she's getting, she still takes time to take care of *me*, too."

After a few minutes where everyone visited, I started the book club meeting. For this club, I felt my job was simply to help move things along, pace-wise, to make sure we got in a full discussion and everyone who wanted to had the chance to participate. I started out by asking about the function of marriage in the book—how did different characters view it? How did it keep some characters (Lydia and Wickham) in line? The discussion started off with a bang and I didn't really have to step in much for the rest of the meeting. Almost everyone seemed to have enjoyed *Pride and Prejudice* and the two that didn't were good-humored about it.

When the book club time was up, I thanked everyone for coming and then stepped back out to the circulation desk, leaving the club members to continue catching up. Sadie Stewart walked up to me with Lynn and a stack of board books in her hands. She looked absolutely worn-out but still managed to smile at me. "Someday, I'll have time to read again, myself."

I smiled back at her. "Life is like that, isn't it? There are times when all we can do is to just get through the busy days and then times when it slows down a little bit for us to do more of the things we want to do."

Sadie grinned. "You must have been speaking with my mom if you know how busy I am! I forgot you're the one who moderates the book club."

"She's a great lady. I love having her in the book club and she really appreciates you driving her here," I said. "She was telling me about all the things you do to help her and how busy you are."

Sadie said fondly, "Mom is my biggest cheerleader. Actually, my *only* cheerleader. But she helps me out too with Lynn. She would do anything for us and I can use somebody like that in my corner. I don't know what I'd do without her help. Even though she stopped driving recently, she's still able to help out a ton. Driving would help, of course, but first she had problems driving at night. Then it was driving in the rain. Finally, she lost confidence in her driving altogether. Actually, I need to help her sell her car, but I've been so busy lately. Mom does a great job keeping an eye on Lynn so I can run errands. And since she's a former teacher, she can even provide Lynn with a little early childhood education. She certainly is doing a better job than Lynn's father ever did." The last words came out bitterly.

I said, "I'm so sorry he treated you both so poorly."

Sadie nodded and sighed. "He did. I was just telling the police chief about it yesterday. He *did* know Lynn was Roger's, but I guess that's his job to track details down. I told him I was furious with Roger for not helping with Lynn but the last thing I would do is murder him. Then I wouldn't have a hope of persuading him to part with any money."

I said, "Did Roger seem as if he was going to come around and help you out? Louise was telling me about Lynn's hospitalization and all the bills."

Sadie gave a short laugh. "When it rains, it pours, right? The poor little thing was so sick. And then, later, *I* was so sick when I got all those bills and I knew I didn't have a hope of paying them off by the time I was supposed to. I felt like Roger had some responsibility for that, you know? But I wouldn't hurt him. When I saw him Friday, he was alive and well."

I drew in a quick breath. "Sorry, but didn't you say you *didn't* see him on Friday?"

Sadie frowned and then said slowly, "If I did, I misspoke. I was briefly there to make a pitch for money . . . yet again. I'd received another big bill, and I really felt like I was drowning. I dropped by his house on the way to pick up Lynn at daycare."

I said, "While you were there, did you see or hear anything that might give a clue as to who killed Roger?"

Sadie thought about this for a moment. "I did see Heather pull up in her car as I was leaving. I didn't even think about that. I was in such a fog of anger when I left after Roger refused *again* to help out. But yeah—I recognized her car. It just didn't seem important at the time at all."

"By the way, did you hear Mary Hughes has been murdered?" I asked.

"What?" Sadie's mouth dropped open a little, and she quickly snapped it shut. "The woman who worked with Roger? *Murdered*? Do the cops think it's connected to Roger's death?"

I said, "I don't know, although I can't imagine it wouldn't be. Whitby isn't exactly rife with murderers. And nothing was stolen from the salon, so it didn't seem like a robbery."

Sadie looked thoughtfully at Lynn, who was pretending to read the board books on the floor, her small finger tracing the words as she'd likely seen her mother do. Then she said, "This is getting crazy. I'm sure the chief is going to come back and talk to me again."

"He might want to know where you were early this morning," I said in an apologetic tone.

"Work," she said with a sigh. "I had to cover for someone's early shift today and the gym opens at five o'clock for all those folks who like to come in before work. So I'll be able to tell him I was at work with lots of witnesses."

"What do you do with Lynn that early?" I asked.

"Oh, there's a nursery at the gym that the employees can use for their kids. It's not all day, though, so I have her over there early and then I have to leave later to take her to daycare. It's not ideal but then I don't usually have the early shifts. So Mary was murdered early *today*?"

I said, "Early this morning, yes. Did you know her?"

Sadie shook her head. "No. That is, I *felt* like I knew her because Roger talked about her a lot. I guess you've heard by now that Mary wasn't Roger's favorite person."

"I got that impression," I said dryly.

"She blamed him for everything that was going on in her life. It really bothered Roger because she was so vocal about it. And you know—when people hear things like that, it could make them think of Roger as less trustworthy. And when you're dealing with someone's money, you want to make sure you inspire trust," she said.

"So, Roger was upset about her bad-mouthing him around town," I said.

"Yes. In fact, if Roger was still alive, I'd say he'd be suspect number one in Mary's murder," said Sadie. She looked across the room. "Looks like my mom is finishing up so I should go. Thanks again for the book club. It's one of the highlights of her month."

Chapter Fourteen

Fortunately, the library became a little quieter after book club let out and after the flurry of checkouts that happened after book loving club members were released out in the stacks. I saw Fitz had curled up asleep with an older man who was reading a magazine and was dozing on and off himself by the fireplace.

About an hour from closing time, I saw another man come in. Fred usually came to the library right after work, still wearing his suit and tie. He had a briefcase full of work, as always. He'd told me before that he got a lot more caught up with his work at the library than he did at home—his house was too distracting and he lost focus. I could pretty much count on him like clockwork.

I remembered Fred worked in the financial realm, but couldn't remember if he was a banker or in investments. I walked over to where he was setting up—in the back near an outlet for his laptop. He looked up when I approached him and gave me a friendly smile.

"How's it going, Ann?" he asked. "If you're going to give me another book recommendation, you should know I'm still working on that World War Two story you gave me."

I smiled at him. "Well, it was a big book. You shouldn't have any trouble renewing it since it's not a recent release. No, actually, there was something else I wanted to ask you about."

He put down his papers and sat back in his chair to more fully focus. "That sounds serious. Okay, shoot."

I said, "It's about Roger Walton. I was wondering if you knew him—or maybe even worked with him. I know you're in finance, but I can't remember exactly what you do."

Fred sighed. "I did hear the news about poor Roger. And yes, I did work in that same office. The new police chief came in recently and asked us a bunch of questions. I actually got to know Roger pretty well since there weren't many of us in the office. I'm a little surprised *you* knew him, though. Roger didn't seem like the sort of guy to hang out at the library. At least, I never saw him here."

I said, "No, I never did, either. One of my patrons was a relative of his and set us up on a blind date."

Fred thought about this for a moment and then slowly shook his head. "Nope. Can't see the two of you together at all. Not to speak ill of the dead, but that wouldn't have worked out."

I said, "The more I learn about Roger, the more I have to agree with you. Unfortunately, I was the one who found him . . . it was the night of our date."

Fred winced. "That sounds like a nightmare."

"It was, even though I didn't know him at all. And a friend of mine might be considered a suspect. I'd really like to clear my friend's name."

Fred nodded. "I can get that. So, what do you want to know?"

"First off, I heard he'd given one investor bad advice," I said.

He chuckled. "I'd say he gave many more than one really bad advice."

"Was he bad at his job?" I asked.

"Not really. I mean, *I've* given bad advice, too. We do the best we can with forecasts for different stocks or funds. But we're not fortune tellers. We have no idea if the market is going to crash or have a setback or whatever. I didn't mean to say Roger didn't do a good job. There were many *more* investors who were pleased with his advice and gained steady earnings," said Fred.

"There was one client who was particularly unhappy with his advice," I said.

Fred considered this, nodding his head. "I think I remember. An old fellow, wasn't it? He came to the office and really let Roger have it . . . on more than one occasion, I believe."

I said, "I'm actually friends with the client. He seemed to think Roger had ruined him almost on purpose. That it was a dereliction of duty or that he was totally heedless."

Fred snorted. "Sorry, but that's simply not true. It was a market fluctuation, that's all. I gather he lost a lot?"

"A lot," I agreed.

"Well, I will say Roger shouldn't have had him put all of his eggs in one basket, no matter what. Especially at his age," said Fred.

I said, "Did you hear about what happened with Mary Hughes?"

Fred nodded. "I heard it on the radio this morning. Awful. I simply can't believe it. Are they saying it was a robbery?"

I shook my head. "No. There is nothing of value there. It definitely seemed to be an attack on Mary."

Fred sighed. "I liked Mary, but she could be a tough person to be around. She continually thought she was getting the short end of the stick at the office and that she was being held back because of her gender."

"Was she?" I asked.

"No. She was being held back because she was difficult. Mary was super smart and had a good track record with investments, but she was prickly. She also liked to gossip. I'd always make sure I never made any personal phone calls at the office where Mary could overhear them. Otherwise, the next thing I knew, Mary would be giving me a card signed by everyone in the office that they hoped my mother was feeling better soon. That kind of thing. I know she meant well, but I didn't like the thought she was listening in on my conversations."

"Was there anything else that held Mary back?" I asked. "Like Roger?"

Fred smiled. "You *have* been looking into this. But what else could you expect from a reference librarian? You're right—Roger got the promotion Mary felt she deserved. And honestly, truth be told, I thought Mary deserved that promotion, too. Roger was *also* difficult to work with. Mary had been there longer and had a better track record than Roger did."

"Can you explain why Mary may not have gotten the promotion?" I asked.

"Roger told some sort of madcap story about Mary. I don't even know what it was, but it could have been anything—that she was accessing sensitive files? That she was pilfering a little on the side? Whatever it was, it not only kept Mary from getting the well-deserved promotion, but it resulted in her being fired from the firm," said Fred. "And she did *not* take that well. As a matter of fact, I'd have thought Mary might have killed Roger. But now it doesn't make sense that Mary was murdered, as well."

I glanced at the clock. "If you're going to get all your work done, I'd better let you get started. But thanks, Fred, you've been a big help."

I started walking away and then Fred gave a little yelp, which made me turn around. He was looking at Fitz with an astounded expression on his face. "A cat!" he said, in the same tone one might use to say 'a baboon.' Fitz was brushing against Fred's pants leg and curling around him.

"Sorry," I said, wincing. "We acquired a cat since the last time you were here. Do you not like them?"

"I do," he said weakly. "I love animals, of course I do. It was just a surprise, that's all. Kitty-kitty?" He reached down a tentative hand and Fitz jumped up on the table to curl up like a centerpiece next to Fred's laptop.

I walked away smiling as Fred became the latest victim to be sucked in by Fitz's charms.

The next hour was completely consumed by a patron who was trying to locate some long-lost relatives without a computer at home. This was harder than it seemed because the last name of the people the patron was trying to find was Smith. Fortunately, by the end of the hour, I'd had some luck, and she walked away smiling.

Luna walked up to my desk and gestured for me to follow her. I did and saw Fitz in the children's area, sprawled out in a child's lap as the child read to him.

Luna said, "This cat isn't for real! I've heard of kids reading to dogs, but kids reading to *cats*?"

"We need to take pictures of this," I said.

"Because no one will believe us if we talk about it," muttered Luna.

Wilson walked up to see what we were looking at. His face lit up at the sight of Fitz and the little boy with the book. "Pure marketing gold," he said. "Look, Ann, you need to be taking pictures when you see scenes like this. We need content that will keep our community engaged."

"Fitz was already a hit on social media when we started the naming contest. Now that people have met him, it's good to keep updating his library activities online," I said.

Wilson said. "Fine. I do have one big concern and I'm open to ideas on how to handle it."

"I'm vacuuming a couple of times a day," I said quickly.

"Not the allergies. I'm worried about the bottom line," said Wilson.

Luna said, "Of course. Who's paying for all this?"

I frowned. "Paying for all what?"

"Fitz's food and litter and stuff. Fitz looks like he's the kind of cat who might have a good-sized appetite," said Luna.

I looked over at the cat who was now licking one of his paws while perking his ears as the child read *Thomas the Tank* to him. "Well, a patron brought in a slew of stuff to get us started. Although, you're right, I didn't really think of a long-term plan for his expenses."

Wilson said, "Ideas?"

I was still thinking about Wilson asking me to take pictures of the cat. "How about a calendar?"

"What? A calendar?" asked Wilson, brow furrowed. Luna said, "That's perfect! We'll all take cute pictures of the cat and we'll make them into a calendar. It's easy and shouldn't cost much. Maybe we can even get the printer to give the library a discount or even give it to us for free if we put an ad for them in the back. Then we can use it as a fundraiser to buy supplies for Fitz."

"It's not the end of the year, though," said Wilson, frowning.

"We could make a 15-month calendar or something," said Luna with a shrug. "If I know this cat, and I'm starting to think I do, then there will be at least 15 opportunities to get an adorable picture of him."

Wilson snapped his fingers. "Okay, you sold me. I think it's a great idea. Let's make it happen." And with that edict, he hurried away again.

Luna said, "On a totally different topic, I did have another question for you. Who's that guy over there? The patron who's always here?"

I looked over back into the adult section of the library near the fireplace. There was a man there, a senior citizen who was wearing a suit and reading *The New York Times*. Fortunately, he was holding the newspaper low enough so I could see his face—most of which was covered by large spectacles that gave him an owlish appearance. "That's Linus Truman," I said.

Luna said, "He's been here *every* day. Most of the day."

I said, "He's been here for years. Always perfectly dressed. If you try to talk to him, you'll get a small smile and a polite grunt of acknowledgment. He has a pattern to his days. He starts out with the local paper and ends up with *The Times*. In between, he reads fiction, usually classics, then nonfiction, usually biographies. He leaves at noon on the dot for lunch and comes back exactly 45 minutes later."

Luna stared at the oblivious Linus through narrowed eyes. "I'm kinda fascinated by him."

"Are you?" I asked, frowning doubtfully. Then I realized I'd become immune to being fascinated by Linus because he was almost a fixture. He did the same thing each day, and he didn't visit with the librarians. We all gave him a respectful distance because he clearly wanted to be alone . . . didn't he?

"All I know is, if I wanted information on anything, he'd be the guy I'd go to," said Luna in a decisive voice. "Think about it—he reads *all day*. We're librarians and we can't even read all day."

I'd considered this before. I was very envious of Linus Truman in many ways. I'd have loved to do nothing but read in a library all day. I sneaked a peek at my book whenever I could, which was usually at breaks and lunch until I made it back home. But *all day*? That was a luxury not afforded to thirty-somethings.

"What's his story?" asked Luna.

I shook my head. "Story? I think his story is that he spends all day every day in the library quietly reading."

"Yes, but why? Does he have a family? Is he trying to get in the Guinness Book of World Records for number of books read in a year or a lifetime? What does he think about all the things he reads?" asked Luna.

I said, "Honestly, I have no idea. Linus doesn't exactly engage in conversation with me, although he's certainly polite. The only reason I know his name is because of his library card."

Luna wagged her finger at me. "Ann, this is another mystery. We need to find out more about Linus."

I snorted. "I don't think Linus Truman had anything to do with Roger or Mary. I'm not sure I have the time to investigate anything else." I paused. "Although I strongly suspect he was the patron who left an anonymous note saying the cats belonged to Elsie Brennon. He didn't want to *tell* me they did, so he jotted down a note, instead. But I'm sure it's him."

I froze. Anonymous notes. Surely, he wouldn't have had anything to do with the last one that came in. I glanced over at him again, impeccable in his suit and shook my head. He couldn't have.

Luna said, "I'm going over to introduce myself. After all, I don't know any better, being new, do I?"

I looked at Linus in his suit and tie and carefully polished dress shoes and then at Luna with her piercings and tattoos and questionable taste in attire. The two couldn't possibly be more different. "Good luck with that. Like I said, he goes out of his way to keep to himself. I've seen him give other patrons the cold shoulder. He's very good at freezing people out."

"Which is exactly why I'm perfect for this assignment," said Luna breezily. "He'll realize I'm brand-new here in the library and that I don't realize he's a committed loner. Also, it's very hard to hurt my feelings. Besides, part of my job is to introduce myself to the patrons, isn't it?" asked Luna.

I nodded.

"I'm heading over now," said Luna.

I couldn't help watching. It was like seeing a train wreck happen in real time. I had to admit I was curious as to how Linus would react to this intrusion. Everyone had pretty much left him alone to his own devices at this point. I hadn't even seen Fitz over there yet, but that was probably because he was so entertained with the kids over in the children's section.

I saw Luna plop down in a chair across from Linus and Linus glance up in surprise, stiffening a bit. Then Luna reached out her hand and Linus reluctantly shook it. Luna leaned back in her chair and proceeded to chat in an animated fashion while Linus stared at her in amazement. That's when a patron came up and asked me if I knew how to find information on the school districts in a state they were about to move to.

Sometime later, Luna sidled up to me again as I was pulling a few requested books for the holds shelf. She said, "He's really just a sweetheart, you know."

I said, "I presume you're talking about Fitz the cat and not Linus. Linus appears to be anything *but* a sweetheart."

"He's just had a hard time, that's all. He said when he retired, he wanted to keep up a routine."

I said, "Well, coming to the library every day definitely qualifies for that."

Luna said, "It didn't start out that way. He and his wife moved here from some other town and they set up their *own* routine. They'd read newspapers in the morning and then do some gardening before lunch. In the afternoons it was puzzles with sandwiches. And so on. But then his wife died unexpectedly, and he's been trying to find his way since then."

I sighed. "That makes me feel sorry I didn't try harder."

Luna said, "But I've seen you with patrons—you have a great way with them and you're always friendly and helpful to everyone. I'm sure you gave it a try."

"I suppose there are only so many times I can get a one-word or no-word response to *good morning*," I said. "After that, I think I've mostly just smiled at him when I've seen him. He's sort of become a fixture at the library as much as the circulation desk or the computer room."

"Well, you can think of him differently now. As a resource," said Luna.

"A resource? For what?" I asked.

"For *anything*. That guy reads all day long."

Chapter Fifteen

That night I was the one to close up. I never really minded it. There's something nice about being in there alone with tons of books for company. And now, of course, with Fitz. He seemed tired too, despite all the napping he'd done during the day on various patrons' laps. He was curled up on his cat bed with his tail curled around his nose. I gave him a few long rubs and heard his deep-throated purr as he lazily opened one eye to look at me before letting it drop down again.

This time I felt the same frisson of fear that happened at my house last night. I shrugged it off, irritated. I could sit at home behind closed doors 24 hours a day, but what kind of a life was that? I didn't want to allow the note writer to make me feel worried about living my life.

I was making a quick round to make sure everything was ready for lights-out when I discovered a patron asleep in the quiet section, a pile of books in front of him. I coughed a few times, lightly, and then produced a louder and more serious-sounding cough when he continued gently snoring. He awoke with a start and gathered his books together, dropping one or two on the floor in his panicked retreat. Then I continued my sweep with renewed vigilance, hoping I wouldn't discover anyone else lurking in the stacks. Seeing no one, I vacuumed the library really quickly for cat fur. Fortunately, Fitz, although not a huge fan of the vacuum, seemed to accept it with equanimity. I locked the doors and turned off the lights.

When I got into my car, I reviewed my food options at home. They were decidedly lacking. There was some leftover salad from a couple of days ago with the best ingredients picked out, a mac and cheese from yesterday's lunch, and some sandwich-making stuff (and I'd had sandwiches for lunch today). I decided I would splurge and go out for dinner. It hadn't been the easiest of weeks and I'd been pretty good with my food budget . . . aside from springing for Chinese food with Nathan.

I knew just where I planned on going, too. I remembered Roger's sister, Heather, was a waitress. Furthermore, I remembered I'd seen her in a particular restaurant before. The restaurant Quittin' Time was not exactly haute cuisine, but it was good solid food and you could get a meat and three vegetables for a reasonable price. Besides, I wanted to follow up with her on the fact she'd been spotted at Roger's house on Friday afternoon.

Quittin' Time had been around for decades. It was a family-owned restaurant in its third generation. Although the linoleum on the floors had seen better days and the vinyl covering the booths was torn in spots, the place was always immaculately clean and the service was always prompt and friendly. And, even if Heather wasn't working, I'd still be able to walk out of there with my tummy full and have some leftovers for another meal.

The hostess got me settled into a booth and handed me an old laminated menu. When the waitress came by, I smiled. It was Heather Walton. What's more, the restaurant wasn't nearly as busy as it usually was, so I'd actually have a chance to talk to her.

Heather greeted me with surprise. "Well, hey there! I didn't expect to see you here."

I said, "Usually I'm more of a lunch person, although I'll occasionally splurge for supper." Then I added after some thought, "Technically, I don't eat out all that often. But I enjoy it when I do."

Heather nodded. "I know what you mean. How are things going? You doin' okay after everything that happened?"

I said, "I am. But how about *you*?" I paused. "I don't know how long it takes for . . . well, for the police to wrap things up, but is there a funeral coming up for Roger? I'd like to attend, if so."

Heather gave me a big smile. "That is just so sweet of you! You didn't even really know him. The police have wrapped up, as you say, although it was just yesterday they released Roger. The thing is, he always said he wanted to be cremated, so we're going to follow his wishes."

"It's good he actually stated what his wishes *were*. So many people, especially young people, don't do that," I said.

Heather said, "True. Of course, he was really just talking off the cuff. He had no idea we would be in this position." She blinked hard. "Sorry. Sometimes it just gets to me. I mean, he wasn't the easiest guy sometimes, but he didn't deserve this. He was too young—it wasn't his time. Anyway, my mom and I are going to plan a memorial service, but it might be a while: Labor Day weekend or something. We wanted to pick a time when more of my mom's family could fly in to attend."

"And you're holding up okay? And your mom?" I asked.

Heather shrugged. "Mom's okay, I think, although it's been hard on her. Maybe at her age she's almost gotten used to saying goodbye to friends and family. For me, though, it's a funny thing. Sometimes I'm fine and I'm so busy I don't even have time to think about my brother at all. But sometimes, out of the blue, I'll start crying—like over *nothing*. I was in the grocery store and saw a brand of cereal Roger and I used to love when we were kids. Man, we fought over that cereal! He always seemed to get the last helping." Her eyes grew misty thinking about it.

I said, "I think grief is like that. It just ambushes us sometimes." I paused and then slowly asked, "Living in a small town is pretty tough sometimes. I hate to mention this, but I thought you might want to know someone mentioned you'd been spotted at your brother's house Friday afternoon."

Heather looked startled and then snorted. "I shouldn't even be surprised. Everybody knows everything in a small town. Yeah, I was there. I didn't want to tell the cops that because I figured they'd totally shift all the blame to me and I didn't do anything. I'm my mom's only caregiver and I didn't want to get arrested. I only stopped by to remind him that our mother's birthday was in a few days and that she wanted to see him."

"Was he there?" I asked.

"Nope. Never even answered his door. And I knew better than to call him and leave a message—he never checked his messages from me. I guess he just didn't ever want to be put out or have to change his schedule for his family."

"Is that why you were going by his house again when I saw you? To try again to remind him?" I asked.

"That's right. I just figured the police wouldn't understand." Heather glanced around the room to make sure none of the customers needed a water refill or the check.

I said, "Did you hear about Mary Hughes?"

Heather's gaze sharpened as she looked back at me. "Yes, I did. The cops have talked to me about that, too. And I'm sorry, although I didn't know Mary."

"You'd never met her?" I asked.

"No." Heather shook her head, looking away. Somehow, I didn't quite believe her. "I told the police the truth. That I didn't know Mary. And that I was at home sleeping when she was murdered because I'd been working late the night before and had to close up. I'd wished I had some idea who might have killed Mary, but I'd no idea. After all, like I said, I didn't know her." She paused. "Have you decided what you wanted to eat?"

I'd decided on a burger and fries. In a place like Quittin' Time, it was best to stick with the specialties of the house.

Later on, when I got back home, I let myself in my house and sighed in relief at being there. I put my takeaway bag in the fridge, figuring I could eat the rest of it tomorrow for lunch. The hamburgers at Quittin' Time were the size of giant pancakes.

Although I never really found the library very stressful, I'd learned it was good for me to have clear boundaries and markers as to what constituted home life and work. I turned on some soft jazz music to tell myself it was time to relax. Then I poured a glass of wine and picked up my book. Finally, I had a chance to finish reading *The Alchemist*. I'd thought I'd have finished up days ago, which just goes to show how crazy the last few days had been.

I finished the book in no time and then pulled out my computer to pull up my reading log and record my thoughts about the book while it was fresh in my mind. I liked to have a variety of books to read because I had a variety of patrons and was regularly asked what I'd enjoyed reading lately. As usual I wryly realized my nerdiness over books was likely another reason why I wasn't in a relationship. Sometimes I felt like I was in such a major relationship with books that there wasn't a lot of room for anything else.

The only problem was I didn't have anything next on my list I could immediately jump into. Then I remembered the reason I didn't was because I was going to try to read a new release next. I listened to a couple of book-related podcasts for readers and jotted down notes on different options, making a list of books to look up the next day.

Then I glanced at my clock and blinked at the time. How had it ended up being after midnight? This shocked me enough to hurry through the motions of getting ready for bed. I guess I'd started everything late, considering I'd had to close up the library for the night. I hadn't looked at the time once since then and I had the feeling I'd be regretting it the next morning. I regretted it earlier than that when nightmares woke me up again.

When the alarm went off, I awakened, super-groggy. Regardless, I took the time to stretch for a few minutes as a warmup. I got showered and dressed really quickly so I could have a decent breakfast instead of just a granola bar. Luckily, I had enough time to make a breakfast sandwich of avocado, Ranch dressing, sliced hard-boiled egg, and some thin provolone cheese. In the final remaining minutes, I hastily pulled out my leftovers from the night before and threw in a banana. It was a weird combination, but at least I shouldn't be hungry.

I managed to get to the library right on time, although usually I arrived there so early that today I felt late. I ended up entering with some patrons who were quietly waiting in line for the doors to open.

"Late night?" murmured Wilson, raising an eyebrow.

I snorted. "Yes, but not like you think. This late night involved finishing a book and finding another to read."

"Exciting stuff," he said wryly.

I was surprised to see that my famously private patron, Linus Truman, was entering the library with me. Usually he came a bit later in the morning. Maybe Luna had really shaken him up and he was abandoning his routine.

A minute later, I was even more startled when he responded to me when I told him *good morning*. Now seriously unnerved, I watched him until he settled down in his usual spot with the newspaper. It was good to see not everything had been completely turned on its head.

Luna was in bright and early this morning. What was more, she had her mother with her. I greeted the lady, and she gave me a tight smile in return as she pushed her walker grimly ahead of her.

Luna carefully got her mother set up in the comfy chairs in the periodical section. She walked over to the magazines and peered at them for a few moments before hesitantly pulling out a few and putting them on the table next to the chair. Then she plugged in her mother's laptop and cell phone and handed her mother the knitting she was working on.

"Mercy!" said Mrs. Macon crisply. "I don't need as much stuff to do as you think! I told you I'm only spending a little while here."

Luna's voice was surprisingly meek. "I know, Mama. I just want to make sure you're comfortable and have everything within reach. If you need me, just text me—don't try to get up and walk over to the children's section. I'll be right over."

"I'm sure I'll be fine," said her mom shortly. She picked up her knitting pointedly.

Luna sidled up to me and said in a low voice, "She's kind of a bear this morning, but I got her here."

"Good," I replied fervently. "Maybe a change of scene will do her good."

"It sure can't hurt," said Luna. Then she paused. "Unless she's so miserable that she decides never to leave her house again."

I shook my head. "I don't think that's going to happen. Did you mention the film club to her?"

Luna grimaced. "I did. I think her response was *harrumph*. I'll be surprised if she goes. But she knows the time and the location, just in case."

A little later that morning, my old professor, Nathan, walked into the library and right up to me at the desk.

"Good to see you this morning, Nathan," I said, smiling at him.

He smiled back. "Yes, I thought I'd just check out a couple of books on gardening. I'm going to expand my garden and wanted some fresh ideas."

"It's hard to imagine you don't already know everything there is to know about gardening in this area," I said. Nathan had created a beautiful garden at his old house—with beautiful shrubbery and flowers and a vegetable garden, to boot. His wife had also been a gardening enthusiast. "In fact, I was going to ask *you* some questions about what to add to my garden. All I've been doing lately is just keeping up with the weeds and watering the plants. My great-aunt was such a genius with gardening and I don't want to destroy her legacy."

"From what I've seen, I think you're doing a fine job keeping all her plants in good health. How about if I come by the house one day soon and take a look at your yard? I can't remember off the top of my head what you've already got planted and how much sun and shade you have," he offered.

"Sounds good," I said with a smile. "I could really use the advice. I owe you one."

"No, we're even. Remember, you paid for the Chinese food the other day."

I said, "Somehow I don't think that's still even. But thank you."

I expected Nathan to give me a friendly goodbye and then head off to the stacks to find the books. But this time he hesitated.

"Anything else you're looking for?" I asked.

He said with a rueful smile, "I was actually curious to hear how the case was going. Have you spoken to Chief Edison lately? The more I think about Roger, the more I feel sort of sorry for him."

I raised my eyebrows. "Sorry for him? After what happened?"

"Yeah, but let's face it—I could have tracked that stock a little better on my end. And I didn't have to be such a trusting schmuck, either. Besides, he was a young man with his whole life ahead of him. What happened to him was a real travesty," said Nathan.

I said slowly, "It's been a crazy couple of days. I received this letter at the library, warning me off from poking around in Roger's death."

"What?" Nathan's eyebrows shot up and then knit together as he glowered at the very idea of someone threatening me.

I told him what had arrived. "It didn't really bother me, except to tell me someone seemed to think I might be dangerous to them." Nathan still looked worried and so I tacked on, "Besides, I'd just had that self-defense course from the chief himself."

"Well, that makes me feel *slightly* better," he said.

I filled him in on some of what we'd learned. "It was a successful class. I wasn't sure how many attendees we were going to have since Whitby seems like such a small, safe place. But we had enough that I'm going to ask the chief to repeat the class again."

Nathan said, "Maybe the fact that there was a murder here drove the number of attendees up."

"That's true. And now there have been *two* murders, so . . ." I saw Nathan's look of surprise and said, "Oh, you didn't know about Mary."

"Not Mary *Hughes*! We were just talking about her."

Chapter Sixteen

I said, "I'm afraid so. I got confirmation from Burton that it was definitely murder."

"But why would anyone do such a thing? Could it possibly be a coincidence? Could she have someone in her life who wanted to do away with her and just chose this time to do that?" asked Nathan.

I said, "It certainly seems like it must be connected in some way to Roger's death. The only thing I can think of is that she knew something about who might be responsible for his murder."

Nathan said, "And then she tried blackmailing this person?"

"That's what I'm thinking. I spoke with a woman Mary worked with, and she said Mary had hit a rough patch, financially speaking. It could be that she tried to use what she'd seen or knew about to pressure someone into giving her money," I said.

"And that person thought it would be more expedient to get rid of her than to keep paying her," said Nathan.

"And possibly more and more as time went on," I added.

Nathan said, "Ann, this is serious. Someone is getting shaken up."

"Maybe that means I'm getting closer to the truth," I said lightly. "Just like my mentor, Nancy Drew."

"I don't want you to get hurt," said Nathan in a stubborn voice I'd never heard before. "Seriously. I think you should drop it. It's less of a cerebral exercise and more dangerous than it was at the start. You've been threatened. There's another life lost."

I reached out and squeezed his hand. "Thank you for looking out for me. I promise I'm not going to do anything stupid. You know how much I value my own safety. I'm just asking a few questions."

Nathan sighed. "I didn't think you'd *do* anything stupid. You're a reference librarian. You're too smart to be dumb." He paused. "Well, if you insist on continuing to ask questions, let me go ahead and tell you what *I* was doing at the time Mary was murdered."

"What were you doing?" I asked. I hoped he wouldn't answer.

He grinned at me and I felt a sense of relief. "Trick question, right? I don't *know* what time Mary was murdered because you didn't tell me and I didn't know about it."

"It was first thing in the morning," I said. "Mary was killed where she worked—at a tanning salon in town."

Nathan said with a twinkle in his eye, "First off, I think somebody would notice if I walked into a tanning salon. I don't fit the profile of their usual clients."

I said, "I'd say that's likely."

"But I don't have a great alibi since I didn't realize I'd need one. I was probably either eating cornflakes or walking Mr. Henry," said Nathan thoughtfully.

"Sounds likely," I agreed.

He said, "I didn't, naturally, really know Mary, and she never had anything to do with advising me. She never was familiar with my account. There's just no reason why I'd want to do away with her."

"And she never tried to blackmail you?" I asked lightly.

He flushed a little and then added ruefully, "Good point. I guess that was the direction we were going in, weren't we? That she knew something about the murderer. No, I didn't have any secret meetings with Mary where she tried blackmailing me." He paused. "There *is* something I do know about Mary that might be of interest."

"What's that?" I asked.

"It's actually more about Roger's sister, Heather."

I raised my eyebrows questioningly at him. "I didn't realize the two of you knew each other."

"It's not really a matter of *knowing* each other. It's more that she and I became acquainted when I would be out walking Mr. Henry. I'm something of a creature of habit and apparently Heather is on something of a tight schedule. It just so happened I would see her every day when I'd be out walking Mr. Henry. We'd chat a little about how handsome her little boy is and that sort of thing," said Nathan.

"How did you find out about her connection to Roger?" I asked curiously. "That's the kind of thing that doesn't sound as if it would come up in the kind of small talk you're making."

Nathan said, "I actually *didn't* know about it for a long time. Then I saw Roger getting out of his car one day and approaching Heather when she was about to leave for work. I was planning on warning her off the next day—I figured he was some sort of boyfriend or something. I thought I'd let her know he was bad news."

I said ruefully, "Did you? I bet that was awkward."

"Fortunately, Heather clued me in before it got far. I'd said something the next morning like, 'Say, was that Roger Walton I saw here yesterday?' And she'd quickly made a face and said, 'Yes, he's my brother.' And then I could manage a very pleasant smile and say I hadn't realized they were related and that I'd known Roger through his work."

I asked, "And how does Heather factor into Mary's death?"

Nathan said hastily, "I don't know if she does. I'll say that right up front. But I *did* see Mary at Heather's house just a few days ago. Mr. Henry and I were actually just a few minutes late because he'd found something particularly interesting to sniff and I didn't want to drag him away."

"What did you see?" I asked.

"Heather looked angry," said Nathan with a shrug. "Now I sort of feel as if I'm throwing her under the bus. But Mary was standing there with a self-satisfied expression on her face and Heather's face was flushed and furious. She looked as if she were on the verge of tears, so I didn't wave or try to visit. I'm not sure what was going on. I wouldn't have said those two would even really know each other. Unfortunately, that's all the information I have. I don't know what they were talking about."

I hesitated and then said, "Nathan, I do have one thing to ask you about. When I spoke to Mary at the salon, she mentioned you had been *really* upset about the financial setback you had when Roger gave you bad advice."

Nathan sighed. "Well, that sounds about right. I wasn't *happy*, that's for sure."

"She said you'd really blown your top." I paused. "It just surprised me because I remember how calm you were in the classroom. No matter what was going on, you always were able to keep your cool."

Nathan replied, "That's a different situation. That was my job, and I worked for years to keep myself unruffled even when a student provoked me. No, I'm afraid patience is not one of my virtues. I've worked most of my life trying to make myself a more patient person. Although I'm proud I was able to accomplish this at work, I'm still trying to master it on a personal level. I'm afraid that, at this point in my life, it's a lost cause."

I said lightly, "I wasn't even aware you have a bad temper. You must be doing a better job than you give yourself credit for."

With perfect timing, Fitz hopped up on the counter in front of me. He purred and turned his green eyes on Nathan.

Nathan chuckled. "This must be the young fella you were telling me about. Fitz?"

He reached out a hand and Fitz raised his chin to allow himself to be scratched.

"He's fast on his way to being spoiled rotten," I said ruefully. "But he doesn't act it. He's just super-sweet."

"How is he fitting in here?" asked Nathan.

"Like he's always lived here. Like it's home. He doesn't try to get out when the doors open. He's friendly to everyone, but doesn't seem like he tries to force his attentions on people who aren't interested, either. And he's been amazing so far in the children's section. Luna pointed out that there were children reading to him while he lay in their laps and purred." I snapped my fingers. "Actually, I'm supposed to be catching Fitz at particularly adorable times and taking a picture."

"For posting online?" Nathan rubbed Fitz's back, and the cat gave him a loving look.

"Mainly for a calendar. It's supposed to act as a fundraiser for Fitz's care and feeding," I said.

Nathan pulled his phone out. "I saw something earlier today you should probably see."

He fiddled with his phone for a minute or so and then handed it over to me. It was one of the library's social media sites and there were people commenting on our last post—a post that had a picture of one of our computers and was promoting a basic computer lesson here. The comments were all along the lines of 'where's Fitz in these pictures?'

I chuckled. "All right. Well, I guess the good news is that Fitz is popular. The bad news is that run-of-the-mill photos of computers aren't going to cut it anymore."

Nathan said, "Just think of it as a way to ensure your programs get more shares. If you had a great picture of Fitz sitting in the chair in front of the computer, the post probably would have gone viral."

We smiled over that and then Nathan's face grew more serious again. "You promise you're not going to take any chances?"

"I promise," I said.

After Nathan left me to find his books, I did spend the next forty-five minutes following Fitz around. I didn't plan on it taking that long because I figured Fitz would simply find a good napping location and that would be the end of it.

Instead, Fitz took me on an unexpected journey that led me to the fireplace in the reading area. Fitz rolled on his back and looked fetching as I scattered a few books around him in the background, in the children's area where he curled up with a stuffed version of Clifford the Big Red Dog and purred as kids rubbed him, and deep in the nonfiction stacks where he hopped on a shelf and playfully looked down at me. I hurried to the breakroom and brought back a cat toy that was a fishing pole with a feather hanging on a string that Lisa the storytime mom had bought. Fitz obligingly played with it in an adorable fashion. I felt as though we should have enough material for at least a few months of the calendar and for a few social media posts, too.

Then I watched as Fitz, apparently worn out from all of his cuteness, wandered into the periodical section. He walked over to Mrs. Macon's chair and put his paws up on the chair without jumping. Luna's mom glanced down, smiled the first smile I'd seen since she came in, and patted her lap. Fitz curled up in her lap and fell immediately asleep as Mrs. Macon rubbed him and closed her own eyes.

Luna walked up to check in on her mom and I put a finger to my lips, gesturing at Fitz and her mother.

"She actually looks *peaceful*," said Luna in amazement. "Ever since I've come home, her face has been creased with worry, even when she sleeps. Fitz is a miracle worker." She clamped her hand to her mouth. "I better not say anything more, or I'll jinx it. By the way, I've been looking for you."

"Sorry—I've been getting precious pictures of Fitz for the calendar Wilson wants. What's up?"

Luna said, "I was picking up some food for Mama and me when I saw something interesting."

We paused while a patron asked me where the card catalog was. We hadn't had one in ages, but we still got requests. I showed her how to find books on the library computer and then joined Luna again. "What did you see?"

"Our favorite local physician was out grabbing lunch, too. But again, he was approached by someone in the community. Looks like the poor guy just can't catch a break in Whitby," drawled Luna.

I said, "Yeah, doctors in this town sort of stand out since there aren't that many of them. So, this was Kenneth Driscoll?"

"Exactly. There was this woman, older than you and younger than me, who was trying to get his attention," said Luna.

"What, like rudely? Or calling out to him?" I asked.

"Like rudely. She was being very loud and not caring who might have been turning around to look. Like me," said Luna.

"Was she mad?"

Luna grinned, showing off a gold tooth. "Mad as a wet hen. Told our Dr. Driscoll that he should take a little more care in checking his messages and replying back to patients."

"I'm sure he liked that advice," I said with a smile tugging at my lips. "What was she trying to get in touch with him about? Did she give any lurid details? Waiting on test results for her bloodwork?"

Luna glanced around them and leaned in to say in a hushed tone, "It sounded more like she was having an affair with Dr. Driscoll." She raised her eyebrows for emphasis.

I blinked at her. "Really? That would be tough to get away with here. I feel like all eyes are on the doctor all the time."

"And he's married?" asked Luna.

"Most definitely."

"Maybe that was the thrill of it—trying to get away with something that would be tough to get away with," said Luna with a shrug.

The library was quiet, and I moved to sit behind the reference desk. "I'm going to look him up."

Luna grinned at me. "That's my girl. Although I somehow don't think his affair is going to show up on Google."

"No. But if he has secrets, maybe I don't really know all that much about him. Maybe none of us do. We just see good old Dr. Driscoll whenever we have a problem and we expect everything about him to be the same."

Luna asked, "What *do* you know about him?"

"Honestly? Not much. All I know is that he *seems* good at his job. But what do I know about medical stuff? And he *seems* really arrogant. But why wouldn't he be when he has such an important position in such a small town?" I asked as I scanned the results of his name online. I peered closely at the computer and said slowly, "Well, this is interesting."

"What's that? The good doctor sings drunken karaoke a couple of towns over?" asked Luna with a chuckle.

"No. But the good doctor had a malpractice suit or two against him," I said. I read on for a few moments. "It looks to me like he ran into trouble in Georgia, picked up stakes, got licensed in North Carolina, and then started working here."

Luna said, "I don't think that's illegal or anything, is it? Unless he's been barred from practicing medicine."

"I don't see any sign of that here. In which case, that *would* be illegal. But from what I see here, it looks like he's run into some problems before. I'd think he wouldn't want any more trouble of any kind," I said.

"Like an inappropriate relationship with a patient?" asked Luna, nodding her head.

"Exactly."

Luna nodded. "Got it. Okay, I've got to run—the storytime is about to start. Just . . . that's food for thought, isn't it?"

"It surely is," I said.

That evening I closed up again and then hopped in my old Subaru. The gas gauge was pretty low, and I sighed. Sometimes, with everything else going on, the car was one of the last things on my mind. But I sure wouldn't be in good shape if anything happened to it. I drove to the gas station.

And, wouldn't you know it, Kenneth Driscoll was there. It seemed he was getting out and about from the office fairly regularly these days. Although, to be fair, it was dark outside now.

I started filling up my car, watching as he put the gas cap on his high-end Lexus and walked inside the station. I was debating whether I wanted to go ahead and approach him again after having had something of a contentious conversation while he was volunteering at the library. As I was considering this, another car drove up in a hurry.

A woman with blonde hair in an artful hairdo, hopped out of her sedan. She strode over to the doctor's Lexus, car keys firmly in hand, and then dug her key into the side of the car and scratched the black paint all the way from the front of the car to the tail end. Admiring her handiwork, she then walked to the other side of the car and repeated the process. "That'll teach you to dump me," she hissed in a satisfied voice.

Chapter Seventeen

I didn't say a word. This woman didn't look as if she was in the mood to be messed with, and I certainly had no protective feelings for the doctor.

Without even a glance to see where the physician was or if he was approaching, the woman hopped back into her modest sedan and sped off.

I winced. I had the feeling Dr. Driscoll wasn't going to be very happy to see this. From what I could tell, he took very good care of the car.

The door to the gas station opened, and the doctor appeared, grasping a soft drink. He gaped at his car and then glanced over at me.

I raised my hands. "I had nothing to do with that. But I saw who did."

Dr. Driscoll tightened his lips together and gave a curt nod. He ran a finger lightly over the damaged paint and then unlocked his car with his key fob.

I pulled my phone out of my pocket.

"What are you doing?" he asked.

I frowned at him. "Calling Chief Edison, of course. Your car was vandalized. I saw who was responsible, Dr. Driscoll."

"It doesn't matter," he said with a shrug.

"Of *course* it matters!" I said.

"Look, I don't want to report it," he snapped. Then he took a deep breath and started again. "I'm sorry. I just don't want to get the police involved, that's all. It's probably some patient who is upset I missed a diagnosis or something. Maybe she had to wait too long in the waiting room or the exam room one day. Or maybe she thinks her medical bills are too high."

"And I didn't say it was a she," I noted coolly. "What's more, she was talking to herself—something about you dumping her."

He froze, giving me an icy look, and then slumped against the damaged car. "Okay, you've got me. It's been a long day and I guess I'm not really thinking straight." He glanced around him to make sure we were alone. "The thing is, this woman and I were in a relationship. She wants me to leave my wife. I never gave her any indication I wanted to do so or ever planned on doing so. And she . . . she won't give up."

"She's stalking you?" I asked.

"Or something. It's at the point where she's starting to even come by the house or sit outside. Our affair was a mistake and I don't want my wife to find out. It would only deeply hurt and distress her, and there's simply no reason to do that." His words came out perfunctorily as if he'd either rehearsed them or had spoken them to his lover . . . or both.

I said slowly, "And Roger Walton knew about this."

Kenneth Driscoll again froze. "What do you know about that?"

"Nothing. I didn't even really know Roger. But I do know the kind of person he was, and I haven't really gotten the greatest impression of him. I could totally see him trying to blackmail you over an affair. Although I'm not really sure how he would have found out about it," I said.

Kenneth said, "Who knows? Who cares? He knew about it, and that was enough."

I said, "Did you hear Mary Hughes has been murdered?"

His face was puzzled. "I have no idea who Mary Hughes is."

I said, "She used to work with Roger. Now she's dead."

Kenneth Driscoll gave a short huff. "Well, I'm very sorry to hear that, but I certainly had nothing to do with it. I'm sure I don't have any patients by that name, or any acquaintances. As small as Whitby is, there are still people here I don't know. Why on earth would I want to kill someone I've never even met?"

I took a deep breath. "The thought is maybe Mary knew something about who murdered Roger."

The doctor tilted his head to one side. "You're thinking this Mary character saw or heard something about the previous murder. Then she blackmailed the perpetrator, and they decided to do away with her. Is that right?"

I nodded. "That's the long and short of it."

"Whoever she was, it sounds like she didn't operate in a very smart way," he said.

"How much did you want to cover up your involvement with the woman who just scratched up your car?" I asked.

"Not enough to kill two people over it!" The doctor scowled at me. "Look, I don't really know who you are and I'm pretty sure you don't know who *I* am. I spend the majority of my day, every day, trying to make people in this town feel better. I save lives, I don't eliminate them."

I gave him a tight smile. "I get it. Okay, thanks."

I turned away to get in my car and he called out to me in a panicked voice, "Hey, what are you planning to do now?"

I raised my eyebrows at him. "I'm planning on getting in this car, heading home, and eating an uninspired supper of tuna salad unless I muster the energy to go to the grocery store. It's been a long day."

He glowered at me. "I mean what are you planning on doing with the information you've just found out?"

I snorted. "I'm not planning on blackmailing you over it, if that's what you're saying. I might only be a librarian, but I'm not desperate enough for cash to break the law."

Dr. Driscoll seemed to relax slightly. Then he said, "But you'll talk about it."

"I'm not going to run to your wife and tell her about your affair, but I feel as though Chief Edison should know about it. Besides, I'm not the only person who knows. Someone else told me about an argument you'd had with this woman recently." The last thing I needed was for him to think I was a threat to him: or, at least, the *only* threat.

He said impatiently, "But that's only going to send him on a red herring! It's going to distract him from finding the actual murderer. And he may ask questions that lead to my wife finding out about my affair."

I said coolly, "If you're concerned about your wife, perhaps that's something you should have taken into account before you embarked on the affair."

I got into my car, started it up, and drove away with the doctor staring after me with narrowed eyes.

The next morning when I arrived at the library, there was yet another letter waiting for me. Wilson made a face as soon as he spotted it.

"I'm calling the police," he said grimly.

"I don't think there's anything Chief Edison can do," I said. "He already knows about the first letter. It's not as if I can have an armed guard around me twenty-four hours a day. Besides, I don't really get the sense I'm in much danger." I decided not to mention how freaked out I'd been both at home and at the library at night. That was simply my imagination working overtime.

Wilson frowned at me. "Why not? The letters sound serious."

"The letters sound like someone is desperate but not brave enough to confront me in any way," I said.

"Regardless, I'm calling the chief," said Wilson briskly.

And in a testament to the size of the town, the chief was at the library in only seven or eight minutes.

I was checking out a patron's books when he came in. Wilson said, "I'll take this over. You and Ann can speak in the breakroom, Chief Edison." He handed the policeman the letter, which he'd carefully wrapped in a tissue.

I sighed and led the chief to the back.

He and I sat down at the breakroom table and he skimmed the letter. "This is the second one you've received."

"That's right. It's made my boss pretty unnerved, but I think it's because it's pulled the library into the whole mess. But then, after all, I'm here at the library most of the time," I said.

Burton nodded. "I'll take this with me, although I don't have a lot of hope that we'll find out who's behind this. What this letter *does* make me think is that you've continued to try to get information about the two murders."

"Guilty," I said ruefully.

"I'm not going to tell you no. You're a grown woman, after all, and you can assess your own risks. Just be careful. The last thing I need right now is another problem."

I raised my eyebrows. "You've been busy?"

"Astoundingly, yes. Whitby has lots going on. I'd completely underestimated what I'd be dealing with here. I'd assumed this job would be a piece of cake after the last place I worked. Instead, there are all sorts of things going on that need addressing," said Burton, sitting back in his chair, which groaned in protest.

"What kinds of things?" I asked curiously.

Burton started counting off all the local crime issues on his pudgy fingers. "Chronic shoplifting, car break-ins, speeders, domestic issues, and a fatal accident involving a tree."

I frowned. "I had no idea. Of course, I knew about the accident, since that was big news. But not the rest of it."

"Yes, poor Elsie Brennon," said Burton, shaking his head. "That was pretty much my introduction to the town, too. You probably missed the other stories because you've been so wrapped up in these murders. You'll see it all in the local paper—I know the library carries it."

I nodded absently. "I'll check them out. So, with all of that going on, have you found out anything more about either of the murders?"

"Nothing very big. And I feel like the residents are getting impatient about my making some progress. No one wants to think their town has a murderer running around it," said Burton.

I said, "What makes you feel that way?"

"They're asking me about it—all the time. Just like you just did," said Burton. "The fact is, all I really know is Mary Hughes was the type of person you didn't want to know your secrets. She liked to gossip and tell tales. What's more, I found some evidence while searching her home and computer that she might be a blackmailer on top of it all."

I said, "That definitely makes sense. Why else would someone want to kill Mary?"

Burton raised an eyebrow. "That's what I asked myself. I looked into her family—and they weren't really around anymore. Most of them were dead and the rest of the family she hadn't been in touch with for years. She'd never been married. There didn't seem to be a reason why anyone else would possibly want to murder her."

We both thought about this for a moment until we were interrupted by the appearance of Fitz. He rolled over on his back and looked fetchingly at Chief Edison.

Burton wasn't convinced. "I'm not so sure about rubbing your tummy, buddy. I have the feeling you'd take my hand off."

I laughed. "This cat is as mild-mannered as they come. But I'm with you—I'm not much of a belly rubber when it comes to cats. Maybe just tickle him under his chin."

Burton delicately did this and chuckled when Fitz closed his eyes and started purring loudly. "Well, you sure do have a sweet cat, that's for sure." He paused and then asked casually, "Luna working today?"

"Yes, but she's out for a little while. She needed to take her mother to an appointment."

Burton nodded, but I saw the disappointment flash in his eyes.

I said lightly, "I don't think I've even asked anything about yourself and how you came to be here. Do you have family nearby? What made you decide to move over to the big city of Whitby?"

"No family nearby," he said. "I had much older parents, and I lost them both ten years ago. I was an only child, so no brothers or sisters, either."

"Not married?" I asked. I was guessing the answer to the marriage question was a no, judging from his response to Luna, but you never knew.

"I was married a long time ago, but it didn't go so well, unfortunately. We ended up going our separate ways. The divorce was my fault—I was spending a lot of hours on the job and not enough hours at home. That's not an equation that really adds up to a successful relationship," he said ruefully.

"Did you have children?" I asked.

"I have a son, but he lives on the west coast. I see him as much as I can and he flies over a few times a year. It's not as often as we'd both like, but we keep in touch by phone and online. He's a great kid." He laughed. "Okay, so not really a kid—an adult. But he's terrific." He paused and then asked curiously, "And you don't have a significant other? Not divorced?"

I shook my head. Usually I let it go at that, but there's something in Burton's calm manner that makes me want to tell him things. "I haven't had a serious relationship since one I had in college." I gave a short laugh. "My personal life has always been a mess. I lost my boyfriend, Robert. He was killed by a drunk driver when we were in school."

Burton's eyes were sad. "I'm so sorry to hear that. It's not like you hadn't had enough loss in your life. You're not old enough to have gone through tragedy twice."

I nodded, swallowing to make sure my voice was steady. I didn't ever talk about Robert and didn't trust myself not to be emotional when I did. Not only did I still feel grief over losing him, I also still felt a sense of irrational guilt. He'd been on his way to bring me soup from Panera when he'd been hit by the drunk driver. I'd been sick with a cold and was barraged by exams and he'd picked up soup on the spur of the moment for me. I decided it would be safer for me to ask more questions about Burton instead of being the focus of the conversation.

"And what made you decide to move here?" I asked. "Although it sounds like it ended up being a lot busier here than you were expecting."

He chuckled. "Oh, I wanted a slower pace. Now I'm kind of laughing about that. I was the chief in a bigger town and it seemed like every day I was absolutely drained by the end of the day. I started looking out for something a little quieter and saw an opening here. Of course, the fact that there's a lake and mountains and rivers and beautiful old buildings made it an even easier sell. So here I am."

"I hope you'll enjoy it here," I said. "I really think the spurt of busyness is just temporary. Soon, it will be back to being slow paced again."

"Well, in case it isn't, you've had a self-defense class," he said wryly. "Just keep your wits about you and you'll be fine." I nodded, although my mind was with those newspapers. I wanted to read more about the car accident, which I'd forgotten about until the chief mentioned it.

After leaving Burton, I settled at the circulation desk and opened up my browser to the local newspaper. Since I'd found Roger's body, I hadn't done more than give the paper a cursory glance every morning. I sighed. The newspaper's website was down. This was a fairly typical problem there, which served as a constant annoyance to me. Patrons who weren't subscribers frequently asked me to print out a copy of a wedding announcement or an obituary. Frequently, I was in the position of having to dig out the physical copy of the paper and make photocopies of it.

I got up and walked to the periodicals, helping a patron find a book along the way. I sifted through the stack of archived copies to find the original story about the fatal car accident. It was several days before Roger had been murdered. I carried the newspaper back to the circulation desk and read the story through. It was written as a tribute to Elsie Brennon, who'd been 85 years old at the time of the crash and had lived in Whitby her entire life. It had been rainy that night, and it was a stretch of road where there were no streetlights (not that there were many in Whitby, anyway). Elsie, on her way home from a church potluck, had apparently lost control of her car on a curve and hit the unforgiving bulk of a large tree near the side of the road.

I sighed. There was really nothing there to suggest anything other than an accident. Then I frowned. This was only the newspaper version of the event—the reporter would hardly have known any details. And, for *The Whitby Times*, the accident would likely have seemed cut and dried—an elderly driver, a dark and rainy night, and a treacherous curve.

I hesitated and then pulled out my phone to dial the chief.

"Long time no see," he said dryly when I identified myself.

"I know, sorry. It's just something you said really made me think," I said.

He said, "Can't imagine what that was."

"It was when you were talking about how busy you'd been and all the different issues you'd been dealing with in Whitby. You mentioned the car crash," I said.

"Right," agreed Burton cautiously.

"It's just that you said that the accident was 'something you had to deal with.' Most car accidents aren't exactly investigations that take up a lot of time, I wouldn't think," I said. "Especially this one. It would have seemed more like a tragic accident that occurred in bad weather conditions." I saw a couple of patrons walking by and I moved to the other side of the desk to make sure our conversation was private.

Burton sighed. "You're going all Nancy Drew on me again."

"I was just wondering if maybe it *wasn't* a tragic accident," I said. "Or that it wasn't that Elsie had some sort of medical event that caused her car to go off the road."

Burton hesitated. "Okay. I'll admit it—that's the direction we're heading in. Although there wasn't obviously another car involved because there was no impact of another car on Elsie's, the car tracks indicate another car likely caused the accident. And we had a witness in town who said there seemed to be one driver who was very agitated with Elsie."

"Who would have been a very slow driver, I'm guessing," I said.

"That's right. At least, that's what everyone who knows Elsie said. Slow and cautious," said Burton.

"But if she had been faced with someone with road rage, she might have been distracted or trying to get away," I guessed.

"Chances are she wouldn't have been driving like she normally would," agreed Burton. "And it seemed like the car hit the tree at a high speed."

"Where exactly did this happen?" I asked.

Burton said, "It wasn't in the middle of town or else we'd have had plenty of witnesses to it. But apparently, some driver was upset with poor Elsie's driving in town and then followed her out away from the rest of the traffic."

"Elsie lived farther out, didn't she?" I asked.

"That's right. It's the old rural route highway. No one really uses it much anymore I hear, since there are faster roads and there's not much out on that stretch of road," said Burton.

"And there were no witnesses." I heard a patron put books down on the desk behind me and quickly said, "Got to go. Thanks, Burton."

Chapter Eighteen

I turned and saw Louise there with a pile of books. She smiled at me but seemed distracted. We chatted a little about the weather while I got her checked out. Then she said quickly, "I'm going to run to the restroom real quick. Can I leave these books here at the desk for a minute?"

"Of course," I said.

"Thanks. I think Sadie and Lynn are still deciding what books they want." And she hurried off. Half a minute later, Sadie and Lynn were at the circulation desk.

I smiled at Sadie. "Ready to check out?"

She grinned back but, as usual, I saw that tiredness in her eyes. "I am. But I've just got a bunch of things for Lynn again. I promise the next time I come in I'll look for something for myself to read, too."

I said, "Maybe you should try a collection of short stories. That way you can unwind at night before you turn in, but you don't have to try to keep up with a bunch of characters or story lines."

Sadie nodded thoughtfully. "Maybe something funny? I feel like life hasn't given me much to smile about lately."

"Have you read anything by David Sedaris?" I asked.

Sadie shook her head.

I said, "Give me just a second and I'll pull out a book of his for you."

"And I'll get started on self-checkout while you're doing that," said Sadie, pulling out her library card and moving toward the scanner.

I walked over to the stacks and hesitated for a couple of moments to decide which book Sadie might like best. Then I picked out *Calypso* and walked back to the desk.

"Let me know if you like it," I said as she thanked me and carefully put the book under the scanner.

I wanted to ask her some more about Roger, but Sadie seemed distracted. This might have been because Lynn was apparently hungry and had started crying. The crying was increasing in volume as Sadie continued fumbling with the books. I quickly offered to check them out myself and she gave me a quick smile in response. Sadie reached down and picked Lynn up and started bouncing her around. As I finished up, I glanced around for Fitz. He'd have been the perfect thing to cheer Lynn up. But I saw that Fitz, although looking in our direction, was sitting in Linus Truman's lap. There was no way I was going to disturb that. I thought again how tough it would be to be a single mom as Lynn continued crying.

Louise hurried up. "I'm so sorry! I was in the ladies' room. You shouldn't have tried managing checkout all by yourself." She reached out for Lynn and swung her off Sadie's hip and into her arms with surprising strength. She gave the toddler a doting look. "What does Gramma's little girl want today? A candy bar?" She dug in her purse and produced a Kit-Kat bar. Lynn smiled through her tears at Louise.

"Mom, you're spoiling her," said Sadie half-heartedly. She looked relieved that the crying had stopped, though.

Soon her little face lit up with a smile through her tears. I found a plastic bag Sadie could hold her books in.

Louise walked over to a bench against the wall and she and Lynn sat down on it, Louise helping Lynn unwrap her candy.

Sadie seemed to be lingering for a moment so Lynn could enjoy the candy. I said, "Did Roger ever talk about Kenneth Driscoll?"

Sadie's eyebrows rose. "What . . . the doctor? I don't think so. I mean, Roger never went to the doctor. He was one of those annoying guys who was never sick. And I don't think the two of them would have been friends."

I said slowly, "Could you see a situation where maybe Roger would know something about someone else and maybe use that information against them?"

Lynn reached into the plastic bag and grabbed one of the board books. She started looking at the pictures as Sadie jiggled her around. "You mean like blackmail? Roger?"

I said quickly, "I didn't know Roger. It just seemed like he might somehow had been putting some pressure of some kind on Driscoll. I wondered if that sounded like something he might do."

Sadie looked thoughtful. "I don't know. I wouldn't have immediately said so, but I also wouldn't have said Roger was the kind of guy who would totally ditch all of his responsibilities. I mean, he never did anything for his mom and then the fact he wouldn't take any responsibility for Lynn, either? I never would have guessed that when I started dating him." She frowned. "I did see the doctor acting kind of weird lately. I just didn't think anything much about it at the time because I was trying to juggle Lynn and some of the books we were returning."

"What did you see?" I asked.

"He was just acting real furtive, which I thought was weird since he was here at the library," said Sadie.

"Furtive, as in he didn't want anyone to see him?" I asked.

"That's right. And he had something in his hand. It was just sort of odd. I mean, almost everyone goes into the library with something in their hand, right? Maybe they're returning books, or they have their laptop with them, or their stuff they need to study for school or for work. I mean, I wouldn't have thought anything of it if he'd just walked right through the library door, holding something. But the way he was acting looked suspicious." Sadie shrugged.

"When was this?" I asked.

"Yesterday? Or a couple of days ago. Real recent. And the other weird thing was that after he went in the building, he came right out again almost immediately. He was still looking around to see if anyone was looking at him," said Sadie.

"Did he see you?" Lynn wasn't exactly quiet, after all. It seemed odd that Kenneth wouldn't have seen them.

"No. I'd realized Lynn needed changing, so I'd changed her in the car really fast. She was still looking at a book and I wasn't talking so I don't think he noticed us." She became distracted again as Lynn resumed wailing now the candy was finished. "Sorry, I need to get her out of here. See you later."

I nodded, feeling distracted myself. It certainly sounded like Kenneth was my anonymous letter writer. I felt somehow chilled by this revelation. Here was someone in a position of trust for our town and he was sneaking around the library to give a local librarian threatening notes? It may be time for everyone to find a new doctor.

I glanced up automatically to greet a patron when I heard the automatic doors swish open after Sadie left. But then I froze. It was Grayson, my neighbor. He grinned at me and headed over to the desk.

"Hi there," I said, somewhat inanely. I pulled myself together. "Good to see you today. Can I help you find anything?"

"Oh, I thought I'd just run in here to escape Zelda from pitching the homeowner board to me again," said Grayson lightly.

My eyes opened wide. "Wait, is she outside?"

"No, sorry, just kidding. But if she *had* been outside, that's just what I'd have done. No, I thought I'd just check out the library since I hadn't made it over. And I could use something new to read, too," he said.

Here I was in more of my natural element. "What kinds of things do you like to read?" I asked. I waited, expecting nonfiction of some sort—maybe an inspirational book by a business leader or a biography of a successful investor.

He said, "Well, I *like* to read everything and cover all the bases. I realize that would make me better-rounded. But the fact is I tend to like to read science fiction. Have any recommendations?"

"Sure," I said, quickly coming around the side of the desk. I paused. "I'm guessing you've read a lot of the modern classics. "*Dune*? Collections by Ray Bradbury? Novels by Ursula Le Guin?"

"I won't say I've read them *all*, but I've read a fair amount of their work. And I've read the *Dune* series," he said as he followed me to the stacks.

"How about *The Man in the High Castle* by Philip K Dick?" I asked.

He frowned, thinking. "I haven't read it, but I swear I've come across it recently somehow."

"Philip K Dick also wrote *Do Androids Dream of Electric Sheep*. And *The Man in the High Castle* has been made into a television series, so you might have come across it there."

Grayson snapped his fingers. "That's it. But I haven't watched it. Thanks, I'll give it a go."

I pulled the book out of the shelves and handed it to him, feeling relieved I'd finally had an interaction with Grayson that didn't involve me fumbling for words. "Sounds like you also need to be set up with a library card," I said.

"As a matter of fact, I do." He grinned again at me and followed me back over to circulation, chatting lightly about our neighborhood and Whitby in general and his thoughts on the town.

I registered him for a library card and then he checked out the book, printing out a small slip of paper as a reminder/bookmark.

"You're all set," I said, smiling at him.

He smiled back at me. "Thanks. And thanks for the help."

A moment of warmth and connection passed between us. At least, I *thought* it had. But then I heard a voice approaching.

"Grayson?" the voice said.

He turned, and my friend Trista immediately slid into his arms as if she belonged there. He hugged her, and she planted a light kiss on his jaw since she was about a foot shorter than he was.

"I thought I saw your car out there." She grinned at me. "Hi, Ann. This is the guy I mentioned to you."

I smiled back at her, even though my heart was somewhere in the vicinity of my stomach. "Grayson and I have actually met. He lives in my neighborhood."

"How perfect is *that*?" asked Trista. "Now we really will all have to grab drinks together soon." She turned back to Grayson. "Don't tell me you're a big reader, too? Somehow I wouldn't have pegged you for it."

Grayson gave her an indulgent smile. "Clearly, you don't know everything about me. I'm a huge reader. I just need to have something to read, and now I do." He turned to me apologetically. "Sorry, I should know, but the last time we spoke, I realized you hadn't given me your name."

I colored a little. It sounded like exactly the sort of thing I'd have done in something of a stressful situation. Apparently, there'd been a one-way introduction. "I'm sorry. It's Ann. Ann Beckett."

"Can we go grab some food?" Trista asked, turning her focus back on Grayson. "I'm starving. I've missed at least one meal today."

"Sure thing," he said with a grin. He looked back over at me, eyes twinkling. "Thanks for your help, Ann. See you soon?"

"See you, Ann!" said Trista.

And they were gone.

I should have known nothing escaped Luna. A couple of minutes later, she was standing next to me. "Dishy guy. Too bad about that vile woman who came in."

I made a face at her and continued entering periodicals into the system. "I don't know what you're talking about."

"Oh, come on, Ann. It was written all over your face," said Luna with a snort.

I quickly put a hand up to my face and said in alarm, "Was it?"

"Don't worry. I think it was only obvious to me. I'm, after all, an expert. I'm a librarian—I'm a pro at reading stories," said Luna dryly. "What's the story *there*? An ex?"

I sighed. "Nope. We finally finished going through a rather drawn-out introduction phase today. He's a new neighbor who I tend to embarrass myself around, that's all. And the woman isn't actually vile at all. We've known each other since college. I have to hand it to Trista—she's a fast mover. He hasn't lived in Whitby very long."

Luna said, "That's the thing about a town like this. You have to move really fast before someone gets there before you do. Although, I have to say that, nothing against your friend, but she looks like the kind of person it's really easy to get sick of. I give that relationship six months. But let's think about what you can do in the meantime. There are plenty of fish in the sea."

"Are there?" I asked lightly. "I hate to tell you this because I realize you're single, too, but I think Whitby has been fished-out. We may have to go farther afield."

"Nonsense," said Luna robustly. "I categorically reject that. After all, you had a date with Roger. He was un-fished."

I said, "Yes, and apparently there were lots of really good reasons for that. I appreciate the sentiment, Luna, but the fact of the matter is I have really horrible luck with blind dates. With, actually, *any* kind of setup. Roger was only the latest in a long string of examples."

"So, you're happily single for now, then?" asked Luna with a sigh. "You're no fun at all. You should know everyone thinks it's fun to set people up on dates."

"It's just, unfortunately, not fun for the people being set up," I said with a chuckle. "Yes, happily single."

Luna hurried back to the children's area to help a patron find where the kids' periodicals were and I glanced at the old newspaper again. Elsie's car accident was horrible, but a better thing to focus on than the fact that the town doctor was giving me threatening letters. Besides, something just didn't seem right about Elsie's accident.

Linus Truman gave a small cough and an apologetic smile, which jerked me out of my reverie. "I'm sorry," I said, shaking my head at myself, "I didn't notice you come up." I colored. Wasn't it perfectly obvious I hadn't noticed him walk up to the desk?

He gave me a tentative smile. "I'm sorry to bother you. It looked like you were really deep in your thoughts. I usually check my books out myself, but I have a small fine and I thought I'd pay it in change instead of swiping my card to pay for it."

"Of course!" I said with alacrity, smiling back at him. I took care of checking out his books and handling his fine. He hesitated, and I said quickly, "Is there anything else I can help you with?" Sometimes patrons were nervous about asking for help. It was a funny thing because that's exactly what I was there to do—provide any kind of help I could.

He said slowly, "I saw from your paper here that you were reading up on Elsie Brennon's accident. At least, that's what it looked like." He quickly added, "Sorry. I normally don't like to invade anyone's privacy by being nosy."

I smiled. "If I'd cared about privacy, then I shouldn't have put the newspaper up here on the circulation desk."

He nodded and said, "I just wondered about it. I've seen you speaking with the police chief. Have they made any headway on her case?"

"Not that I heard," I said. "I'm sorry. Was Elsie a friend of yours? I remember you'd told me she'd owned Fitz and the tabby before she died." I flushed again. "Sorry. I mean, I *believe* you may have left me a note to that effect."

"I did leave the note. And I'm afraid she really wasn't a friend. But she was a neighbor. I wasn't probably the friendliest neighbor, unfortunately. I didn't go out of my way to speak with her."

This didn't surprise me a bit, considering how quiet he'd been in the library. I could tell it troubled him, so I said, "I'm sure she didn't mind. It takes all sorts in a neighborhood. Some people want to chat and others would rather keep to themselves."

"But Elsie, although I didn't really know her well, was a kind woman. And the accident she had didn't ring true to me at all."

"In what way?" I asked.

Linus said, "Let's just say I was quite familiar, as a neighbor, with her driving. I have another neighbor, on the other side, who has a teenage son. He flies down the road, making people and wildlife dodge out of the way. There's a patron who's frequently here who drives like that, too—terrifying. She scares me to death when she's in the parking lot because she flies through it like it was a freeway. Elsie was the sedate driver. She's the one who is barely moving."

"She was always really slow?" I asked.

Linus nodded. "I think even if she'd hit a tree, at her usual speed, she'd have been just fine. I mean, twenty miles an hour would have felt like speeding to her. She drove as if she were in a crowded parking lot, all the time. Maybe ten miles an hour."

I nodded. "The fact the accident happened at a higher speed gives you concern?"

"I'm thinking she must have felt scared or chased. I really can't wrap my head around the fact she would have had that sort of accident," said Linus.

I said, "The chief did say there were signs there was another car there. Tire tracks, for one."

"That makes sense," said Linus quietly. "I'm glad they're checking into it further. I was worried no one was really paying attention. Like I said, she was a nice woman. I didn't think what happened to her was fair."

"The woman . . . the patron you said was driving so crazily in the parking lot. Do you know who she is?" I asked.

He shook his head. "I sure don't. But I've seen you speaking with her before. She has a toddler girl. The mom has curly hair? Tall?"

"Sadie Stewart," I said slowly.

"Not sure. But if you could maybe ask her to slow down in the parking lot, it would make things a lot safer."

He gave me a quick, small smile and then hurried away back to his books.

Chapter Nineteen

A couple of hours later, it was time to set up the community room for film club. I pulled out some chairs and wheeled in the television since the Whitby library was still too old-school to have flat screens on the wall. Then I dodged into the staff room to get the popcorn machine going for the popcorn and then pour it into bags. I also got myself a large cup of coffee.

When I made it back to the room, it looked like the whole gang was there, which made me smile. I could honestly hold film club every single week because it made me so happy. There were plenty of films out there and my group wasn't picky. They were enthusiastic about watching *A Trip to the Moon*, a 1902 French silent movie. They were *also* enthusiastic watching 1961's *West Side Story*. And they had no problem with scary films like *Rosemary's Baby*. I could throw almost anything at them and they good-naturedly took it in stride.

When I walked in the room, I saw Timothy, my nerdy teenager patron, was already settling in. Since he was home-schooled, he could make film club. Honestly, if he hadn't been able to make it, I'd probably have changed the program time because Timothy loved it so much. "Had to come early to pick my seat for this one!" he said with a grin. He was wearing sweat-pants and a top that looked far too big for his lanky frame. Top-ping it all off was a *Jurassic Park* baseball cap. He looked relaxed and happy.

Today's movie was actually an old Cary Grant and Rosalind Russell film, *His Girl Friday*. Timothy reminded me a lot of me when I was his age. I was the old soul of my high school. I thought maybe it was because I'd been raised by my great-aunt, but the truth was I *liked* old movies, old books, and old music. Timothy was the same way. I had no doubt he probably had a tough time trying to fit in with peers, but he'd found 'his peo-ple' at film club. This was one place where he felt he belonged. Besides me, he was probably the other member of the club who would be absolutely delighted to meet every single week.

George walked in and gave Timothy a high five. "Got a good one today. Of course, they're *all* good ones." He put his hands on his hips and looked at me. "Of course, you know I'm going to ask you how your social life is going. I don't want all of your fun tied up in hanging out with film nerds."

I laughed. Usually, I'd bristle if somebody brought up my dating life or lack of it. But with George and me it had been something we'd banter lightly about every month. George owned a typewriter repair shop and still somehow managed to make a living. He must have been getting business off the in-ternet, otherwise I couldn't see how he could survive. Still, he always seemed to be busy working on something, at least from what he told us. "My social life? It's all a soap opera, as usual," I said, without going into details. It was, right now of course, much more of a soap opera than it usually was.

Timothy piped up. "Ann doesn't need to settle for some-body who isn't good enough for her. She just has to find the right person."

I grinned at Timothy. "Right as usual, Timothy."

The room started filling up with my regulars and I chatted with everyone as they settled in. When everyone had taken a seat, I dimmed the lights and picked up the remote.

"I'm excited about today's film," I started and then stopped when the door to the community room opened again. I gave a big smile to Mrs. Macon, leaning on her walker and hovering uncertainly in the door. I'd hoped she'd come in, but I never re-ally believed she'd make it here.

"Thanks for joining us! Everyone, this is Mrs. Macon."

"Mona," she corrected a little tersely. "You can all just call me Mona."

"There's an empty seat just over there." Fortunately, there was an accessible seat available. and Luna's mom hesitantly walked over as the film club members greeted her on the way over. I saw a face in the window of the community room and turned to see Luna, giving me a quick wave and holding up her crossed fingers. As soon as her mother turned around, Luna quickly disappeared.

"I think you're all going to enjoy today's film, *His Girl Fri-day*. At least, I really enjoyed it and can't wait to see it again. I know some of you have already seen the movie."

Timothy, my nerdy teen piped up, "Funniest film ever!"

I was glad to see Mona smiling at his enthusiasm. A second smile for the day! I'd have to let Luna know.

I laughed. "Way to set up big expectations, Timothy. There's plenty of popcorn up here, so feel free to get yourself another bag during the movie if you want it. And without further ado, here's the movie."

I clicked 'play' on the remote and settled into a chair near the back of the room with a pad and paper so I could make some notes to help facilitate our discussion later. Not that our discussion ever really needed *too* much facilitation.

I'd expected the comedic film to go over well with this group and I wasn't let down—they were laughing all the way through. I looked over at Mona, hoping she was being drawn in and was relieved to see a smile on her face. The last thing I wanted was for the film to be a big dud and scare her off for good.

When it wrapped up, everyone clapped.

"Bravo!" said Mona.

George said, "How did they *talk* so fast?"

The film was about a fast-talking editor and his equally fast-talking reporter ex-wife. I said, "I'm not sure. I'm guessing they had to do a lot of takes to get it all perfect."

Timothy had apparently read up on the film. "The director didn't mind if they ad-libbed, either, so that was really cool. Like when Cary Grant's character mentions Ralph Bellamy, who was playing in the movie with him."

They tossed around their thoughts on the film and compared it to some other Cary Grant movies we'd seen.

"That guy had a lot of range," said George.

Mona said, "I still love his romantic lead roles the best." She put her hand over her heart. "*To Catch a Thief*. He was just lovely in that film."

George snorted. "What *I* remember best about that movie is the suspense. But, considering it's a Hitchcock film, that should come as no surprise."

I glanced at Mona, hoping she wasn't offended. George could be blunt. In fact, the whole film club enjoyed engaging in lively debate. I saw her blink in surprise and then mull this over.

"I'd totally forgotten about the whole cat burglar thing," she said thoughtfully. "I guess it's the visual feast for the eyes that I remembered the most. But you're right. He was a great dramatic actor. He was also wonderful in Hitchcock's *Suspicion*."

Timothy piped up, "Okay, yeah, he was good with dramatic roles. But remember all the comedic parts he did."

Mona tilted her head to one side. "I'm trying. But unsuccessfully."

Timothy counted off a few. "*Topper, Bringing up Baby, Arsenic and Old Lace*."

"Like I said, the guy had a lot of range," said George.

The discussion went on for a while longer, with Mona becoming more and more engaged. After we wrapped up, I was glad to see several members lingering behind and engaging in conversation with Mona. They encouraged her to the next meeting, and I was glad to see they weren't their usual, cheerfully pushy selves. Mona was smiling shyly, a good sign.

A few minutes later, I was back at the circulation desk, since frequently some film club members liked to pick up a book or two before leaving. Mona slowly walked up to me, leaning heavily on her walker.

"Thanks for inviting me to go to film club," she said with a smile. "At least, Luna told me it was your idea."

"Did you enjoy it?" I asked. "I thought it was a fun film. Although not everyone is crazy about madcap comedy, of course."

"It wasn't really all that madcap," said Mona. "It was really very clever. And somehow I don't think I'd ever seen it."

I was relieved. "Well, if you'd like to see what else we have up our sleeves, be sure to try to make it next time. We'll have something completely different." And it was. I was looking at doing *The Andromeda Strain.*

"I'll try to be here." Mona looked pleased.

I was walking to the breakroom for my lunch break when I hesitated. Maybe I should head over to Quittin' Time instead and see what business Heather had had with Mary. I had a feeling I knew what Mary had been there about, but I wanted to make sure. Heather had already admitted to me that she'd been at Roger's house last Friday. I had the feeling, though, that Mary had seen an opening for blackmailing Heather.

I sighed at the thought of eating out again instead of eating my homemade lunch, but told myself I'd simply eat my lunch for supper . . . and choose something especially inexpensive off the menu.

I realized suddenly as I walked in that I might be eating lunch out for nothing—Heather might not even be working today or her shift might start later in the day. I was relieved when I spotted her across the restaurant as I found myself a table

Heather seemed a little more guarded this afternoon than she had last time. She probably thought I couldn't mind my own business. I gave her what I hoped was a casual, reassuring smile.

"I'm surprised to see you back already," she said lightly. "You're on your way to becoming a regular! What'll it be today? Another hamburger?"

I laughed. "No, that's way too much food for lunch. As a matter of fact, I think I'll just order one of your appetizers." I hastily glanced down at the laminated menu she'd handed me.

Heather pointed a pink nail at the menu. "If you're like me, I'm usually looking for something cheap but filling. Our taco salad is a lot of food, but a great price."

Relieved, I handed her the menu. "That's perfect, thanks." I saw the place was filling up and hesitated, not sure how to launch right into questioning her again.

"Is something wrong?" asked Heather, raising a questioning eyebrow.

"No . . . well . . . actually, yes. I was wondering if you could answer a question for me. It might sound strange, but it could be helpful in finding out the kind of person Mary Hughes was," I said quickly.

Heather sighed and glanced behind her at a table that looked like it was ready to have its order taken. "Let me guess. Somebody in this nosy town saw me and Mary talking together. And you're curious to know what it was about."

I nodded, clearing my throat. "It's just that the person who told me said it looked as if you might be engaging in an argument."

Heather snorted. "That's exactly what it was. Except the argument was all on my side."

I said slowly, "The thing is, I believe Mary was at Roger's house on Friday. I think she went there to confront him about her job. She'd told me a coworker had informed her of your brother's death, but I found out later that her coworker didn't even know who Roger was. Mary herself must have been there. And, considering the fact Mary was having financial trouble, I'm wondering if maybe she tried to blackmail you because she'd seen you at your brother's house."

Heather's eyes narrowed and then she sighed. "You want to know the kind of person Mary was? I'll tell you. She'd *also* seen that I'd stopped by my brother's house last Friday. It was a totally innocent explanation—like I told you, I was just making sure he remembered our mother's birthday. But Mary was convinced I'd had something to do with Roger's death just because I didn't want her to go to the police about it."

I frowned. "You didn't seem very concerned about *me* when you told *me* about your visit there."

"That's because you're a totally reasonable person. Someone a person can trust. Okay, you might be super-nosy, but I guess that might be an occupational hazard for a librarian. Anyway, Mary was wanting money so she wouldn't go to the cops about it. Money! I told her off and then basically laughed in her face before I went back inside, slamming the door behind me. there you go. That's Mary in a nutshell."

"Got it," I said quickly. Someone who looked like he might be her manager was glancing over in our direction now and I didn't want to get Heather into any trouble.

Heather leaned in closely and lowered her voice. "But I didn't kill her. She wasn't worth it."

Since ordering a meal, having it prepared, and then waiting for the check took a little while, I ate really quickly and rushed back to the library as soon as I'd paid up, still thinking about what Heather had told me. Both Roger and Mary seemed to be pretty rough characters, although they didn't deserve what had happened to them.

I was deep in my thoughts while I was walking across the parking lot to the library and didn't hear a voice call my name the first time.

The second time, I turned around. It was Lisa, the mom who'd taken the tabby cat home with her. My heart sank when I noticed she was toting a carrier that appeared to have a cat in it.

"Thank heaven," Lisa laughed. "I was starting to worry I'd gotten your name wrong and have been calling you by the wrong name for half-a-million storytimes."

I gave her a weak smile and looked anxiously at the carrier. "Hi, Lisa. Good to see you. How are things going with our little tabby?"

Lisa looked at my face and then put a hand up to her mouth. "Oh goodness! You thought I didn't *want* her! I'm so sorry . . . I didn't think about how this looked. No, we *love* her! My daughter thinks the sun rises and sets on her and this little tabby is just so patient and sweet with her. We named her Harper . . . like Harper Lee. I thought she might want to see how Fitz is getting on, you know? Just let her sort of check in with him."

I blew out a sigh of relief. "That's great news. She looked like she was super laid-back, just like Fitz is. Let's let them spend some time in the breakroom together, since we never acclimated Harper to the rest of the library."

I brought Lisa in there with me and she set down the crate while I went out into the library to find Fitz. He was curled up with an older lady in the quiet area and I apologetically picked him up. When I got back in the lounge, Lisa opened the door on the carrier. Harper came tentatively out . . . until she saw Fitz. Then she trotted over and started licking Fitz on his head and nuzzling him. He closed his eyes happily.

"Aww!" said Lisa, putting her hand to her chest. "That just warms my heart! Look at those two!"

We chatted about how Harper was doing in her new home while the two cats bumped their heads into each other affectionately. Then, after about ten minutes, Harper gave a trilling meow to Lisa and walked casually into her carrier. Fitz curled up nonchalantly in a sunbeam and promptly fell asleep.

We laughed. I said, "It looks like Harper had a good visit and now she's ready to head back home."

Lisa said, "We *might* just spoil her a little bit."

I said, "She deserves it! Thanks again for checking back in with us. It was a nice little playdate for both of them."

LUNA WAS WALKING BY on her way to break. "So, how'd things go at film club? I've been dying to ask."

"Didn't you ask your mom?"

Luna made a face. "Yeah, but in the mood my mom has been in, she'd probably tell me it was awful just to be contrary."

I said, "She seemed to really love it. She even engaged in a discussion about Cary Grant's different types of roles. And she said she'd try to come back next time."

Luna said, "Yes!" and gave a fist pump. "You have no idea how relieved I am to hear that. I've been at my wit's end. Seriously. Well, but you know that because you saw how low I was yesterday. Anyway, *thanks*."

"All I did was play the movie," I said, raising my hands.

"Oh, I think you did a whole lot more than that, Ann. You selected it, you've encouraged a good group to attend. And you made sure to facilitate a great discussion, I've no doubt. Believe me, I'm very grateful."

I gave her what was apparently an absent grin. Luna squinted and said, "Okay, something's on your mind. What's up? Did you find out something?"

I wanted to talk to her, at least to tell somebody all the things I'd found out today. That Elsie's death hadn't been a terrible accident. That Mary had indeed been a blackmailer and had even tried to blackmail Heather. That the person responsible for leaving threatening letters for me might be the person in the town people respected the most. But now the library seemed especially quiet and I knew my voice would carry with the acoustics of the old building. Plus, Luna was about to have her school-age kid storytime since it was the middle of the afternoon. I decided I'd just fill her in on part of it. I leaned in and whispered, "I think I know who my anonymous letter writer is."

Chapter Twenty

L una's eyes widened. "Who?"

"Apparently, it's the good doctor," I said in a wry voice. Unfortunately, my wry voice trembled just a hair, destroying the effect I was shooting for.

Luna wasn't fooled by my attempt at sangfroid. "How'd you figure that out?" she asked, hands on her hips.

At this point, a group of young teens came in the door, allegedly to study. Their joking voices created a nice background noise for our conversation to continue. I said, "Sadie Stewart just told me she saw him skulking around the library around the time I received a letter."

Luna made a face. "Well, you know something's wrong with him right there. Who skulks around libraries? That would have made him look suspicious right off the bat."

"He's probably not accustomed to acting that way," I said with a shrug. Then I gave a shaky sigh. "It just really bothers me, that's all. He's in this position of public trust and everyone looks up to him. And then here he is leaving threatening letters. It doesn't exactly fit in with his Hippocratic Oath."

Luna snorted. "You can say that again. That would be more of a Hypocrite Oath. So, what are you going to do? Confront him over it?"

At this, *I* snorted. "You clearly have me confused with somebody else. I'm not the kind of person who confronts people who write threatening letters. I don't think Nancy Drew would have done it, either. There's a difference between keenly gathering clues and disseminating information and being foolhardy. But I know what I *will* do."

"What's that?" asked Luna.

"I'll let the police chief know," I said. And I felt as if a weight had been lifted from my shoulders. "There isn't any real evidence, and it's all just hearsay, but at least he'll know." And, I decided, I could fill him in on everything else, too, even if some of it was simply speculation.

"Right. And then, if anything happens to you, Burton will know who to go after," said Luna. Her eyes narrowed as if enjoying the prospect of vengeance being wreaked.

"The only problem with that scenario is it involves something *happening* to me," I said. This time, my wry voice had no tremors in it whatsoever.

"And I know about it, too," said Luna cheerfully. "Plus, I know I'm going to transfer my mom to another physician ASAP."

"I can't blame you, although it doesn't change the fact that he's an excellent doctor," I said.

"Sounds like I'll just be getting in the car and taking Mama on a little drive to the next town over for appointments," said Luna with a shrug. "Problem solved."

Wilson joined us. "Who's closing up tonight?" he asked.

"I'm doing it," I said. "And thanks for reminding me. I probably need to have another shot of caffeine."

Wilson arched his brows. "Sleepy? That doesn't sound like you, Ann."

"It sure doesn't. But I haven't been sleeping well lately," I said. "And I had a big lunch today."

"Well, get that cup of coffee. And, if you don't mind, do an especially good sweep tonight of the patrons. Last week I almost missed one who was sleeping in the quiet study area." Wilson made a face. "That would have been awful if I hadn't found him."

"Waking up in the middle of the night in a silent library?" I asked. "Sounds like my dream come true." I grinned at them as they laughed.

Later, I was glad I'd had the cup of coffee, and that it had been a large one. It was only 8:30, and the library was deserted. Usually that wasn't the case at all—there'd be some high-achieving high school kids trying to finish up an assignment or someone looking for a job on the library computers after working at the job they were eager to leave. Or there'd be a night owl still reading magazines who'd be surprised it was 9:00.

Tonight, though, there was no one except for me and Fitz. Fitz was already in nighttime mode after a long day of snuggling with various patrons and being adorable. I was shelving a few books in the stacks and Fitz was on a nearby shelf, keeping a lazy eye on me.

Suddenly, I felt an icy tingling run up my spine and the hairs on the back of my neck rose. This time I didn't dismiss my worries. I turned around. I was sure I wasn't alone in the library any-more.

My second thought was: why was this a problem for me? It was still, technically, library hours. A patron might have been running by to pick up a book on hold before we closed. Or re-turning a book that was about to be overdue. But I couldn't convince myself I was overreacting. I remembered Burton had stressed the fact during the self-defense class that it was impor-tant to listen to our bodies—to realize when we had a bad feel-ing about something and trust ourselves. He'd recommended a book to *me* and I'd put it on my list: *The Gift of Fear* by Gavin de Becker.

Plus, there was the fact that the fur raised on Fitz's back.

Chapter Twenty-One

I reached for my cell phone to call the police. Had Kenneth Driscoll decided to come over to the library and confront me in person?

I fired off a quick text to Burton before I heard a woman's voice calling. "Ann?"

I breathed a little easier. It was Louise Stewart. Knowing her, she'd accidentally left something in the library earlier when she'd been in with Sadie and Lynn. She and Sadie certainly had a tough time juggling everything when Lynn had been so upset.

"Louise?" I called, phone still in my hand.

When she rounded the tall bookcase behind me, I saw she was holding a gun.

I froze. Then I said, "Louise, what are you doing?"

Louise's face was streaked with tears, but her eyes had a fiercely determined, almost fanatic expression in them that I'd never seen before. As always, she wore her cheerful bright-colored top and pants and chunky necklace, which looked remarkably out of place with the gun.

"I'm keeping my family safe, Ann." Louise's voice was steely.

"No, you're not," I said in as steady and reasonable a voice as I could muster as all the bits and pieces of all the things I knew suddenly fell into place. "What you're doing is *endangering* your family. You're going to have one more death on your conscience and on your record. Instead of being responsible for two homicides, you'll be responsible for three." I paused. "And I would have added a manslaughter to boot, but I think Sadie was responsible for Elsie Brennon's death, wasn't she?"

Louise narrowed her eyes impatiently. "This is all your fault, Ann. You're the one who was snooping around. And the police won't know a thing about it. They haven't so far; why would they catch on now?"

"And you think Burton Edison is a stupid man?" I demanded. "Because let me assure you that he's not. Maybe he has his hands full right now trying to adjust to a new town and get to know everyone. But sooner or later, he's going to figure out that you're the one behind these deaths."

"Like you did?" asked Louise. She said it in almost a reasonable voice.

"That's right," I said calmly. Although my head was spinning. I wished I'd put two and two together just a little faster than I did. "Sadie was the road rage driver. We had a complaint from another patron recently about her reckless driving in the parking lot. You mentioned yourself that Sadie made you nervous when you rode with her. Elsie Brennon was not known for speedy driving. And obviously, Sadie takes things a little too personally when someone slows her down."

Louise said coldly, "Sadie has a lot going on. She works all day and then picks up Lynn, drives me around, and runs all the errands that she can't do during work hours. If you think that's easy, I can assure you it's not. Sometimes she gets frustrated when people get in her way and slow her down."

Right now, I'd agree with her about anything. I just needed to keep her talking. "I'm sure you saw plenty of instances of road rage when you rode with her. And when Elsie Brennon held Sadie up that night, she couldn't let it go, could she? She followed her out on the rural highway in the dark to make sure she got the message. Did she tailgate her? Honk at her? Whatever Sadie did, it ran her off the road. Because she was trying to get away from her."

Louise's eyes narrowed. "That old woman shouldn't have even been driving anymore—she was a danger to everybody. She should have been more like me and simply stopped driving altogether. If she'd been a better driver, she wouldn't have gone off the road."

I felt a shiver go up my spine at Louise's total callousness. To her, *Sadie* wasn't the danger. The danger was the person who'd gotten in Sadie's way and was, in Louise's eyes, culpable.

Realizing this same callousness was going to be applied to me if I didn't keep her talking, I continued. "And then the problem with Roger. What made you decide to kill him? I could tell you were frustrated with his refusal to help support Lynn. That must have really upset you. There Sadie was, doing all this work, all this driving. And Roger wasn't helping out at all. It wasn't fair, was it, to make Sadie handle everything? She had her hands full already with Lynn and you and work and the bills. And he was throwing it in her face, wasn't he? He knew he could get away with not helping because she didn't have the funds to take him to court to get child support," I said as I edged closer to Louise, hoping I could get in range to kick the gun out of her hand. I kept speaking to her in a soothing voice. "You went over there Friday night just to talk to him again, didn't you?"

"Too bad he wasn't in the mood for talking, since he had a *date*." Now that frisson of anger was back. I was unhappy to note that it was directed at me.

Louise's expression was icy. "He didn't just refuse support. He demanded money from me." She gave a short laugh. "I'll give you a moment to figure that out."

My eyes opened wider. "He knew about the car accident. He'd witnessed it? Sadie wouldn't have told him about it. What did he do—try to blackmail her . . . and you?"

Louise said thickly, "When he threatened me, it was all over. I'd had enough. I'd had enough of his disrespect of Sadie, Lynn, and me. I was tired of his lack of support. And then he had the gall to threaten me? My family?"

"How did he threaten you?" I asked. I noticed Fitz's eyes were narrowed and glowing as he stared at Louise from the shelf.

"He saw what happened with Elsie and Sadie," Louise said, eyes glittering dangerously. "Sadie had finally gotten Roger to agree to meet her to talk about Lynn and the help she needed. They were apparently going to meet after work at this Mexican place that was on the way out of town. He was a couple of car lengths behind her. Or so he said."

I said in an even voice, "Roger told you about this. Sadie didn't tell you about the accident?"

"No. I'm sure she'd be devastated to think I knew about it. She hasn't said a word to me, although I can see with my own eyes how exhausted she looks and how anxious this incident has made her. Roger called me on the phone Friday and said he'd just seen Sadie. He told me in great detail about Sadie's incident, taking a lot of pleasure in informing me. He had taken pictures and a short video of what happened after the accident. He said he'd tried to force Sadie to pay him not to tell the police about it, but she didn't have any money. That's why he called me. He knew that, even though I wasn't loaded, I had a lot more than Sadie did. He was an opportunist in every way," spat Louise.

Where was the cavalry? What was taking Burton so long? I had to keep Sadie talking as long as I could.

I said slowly, "So you went over to Roger's house. Despite the fact you don't drive."

Louise shrugged. "Except in the case of emergencies. This was an emergency. I could *not* let Sadie end up in jail."

"You told him you'd bring money. But instead, you murdered him and deleted any incriminating photos or videos from his phone. Because, as Sadie told me, you'd do *anything* for your family. You said yourself that the Stewart women would do anything for their babies. You dote on Lynn and are determined to protect your daughter." I paused and said with more calmness than I felt as I tried to stall for time, "You're a lot stronger than you look. I saw you easily swing Lynn up off Sadie's hip at the circulation desk. You were really adept with that skewer."

"I had to get rid of Roger. The blackmail would never have stopped, Ann. He'd have gone on and on until he milked me dry. Until there was no more money for activities for Lynn or any other extras." She smiled. "I bet you didn't know that I was on my way to becoming an Olympic javelin thrower until I became pregnant. It was the same motion with the skewer—it was almost like muscle memory."

"Unfortunately, however, someone else knew you'd been there and figured out that you must be the one who killed Roger. Mary Hughes had had a busy day. She'd gone over to confront Roger about her own financial issues and saw you and Heather coming and going while she was waiting for Roger to have a free moment to talk to her. And because of those financial issues, she saw a money-making opportunity. She thought she'd attempt a little blackmail. You were an especially good candidate because she must have caught you right after you'd murdered Roger. Heather, on the other hand, had just driven up, tried the doorbell unsuccessfully, and left again. But she *really* had some dirt on you. What did she say when she entered the backyard?"

"Not much. She pulled her phone out like she was going to call the police. I just froze. All I could think about were Sadie and Lynn and what would happen to them if I couldn't help take care of them anymore. Then Mary gave me this mean smile and put her phone back and walked away to the front of the house. I left a moment later," said Louise.

I said, "Then, at some point, Mary got in touch with you. Between Roger and Mary, you must have felt surrounded by blackmailers. You must have told her the same thing you told Roger: that you didn't have any money to spare. But she kept threatening to expose you to the police," I guessed.

"Which scared me. But it didn't make me have more money," said Louise.

"So you decided to get rid of her. Because, again, the blackmail would never have stopped."

Louise didn't say anything. She continued her firm hold on the gun.

"The doors were unlocked, and you killed her with whatever was close to hand, which was apparently a heavy doorstop. Then you hid her body so she wouldn't immediately be found, to help give you time to get away. As for me?" I paused so I could swallow. My throat was so dry. Where was Burton? Surely, he didn't turn off his phone at night or at dinner, did he? Weren't small-town police always available?

Louise's voice became higher pitched and louder. "As for you, I'm really disappointed. Now who's going to recommend library books for Sadie and Lynn? And what about my book club?"

I put my hands up in a calming gesture. "Louise, there's no need for that to change. Luna or I can keep showing Lynn and Sadie good books. The prison library has a program that links to our library . . . but you know what needs to happen next. You can't go on like this, killing people to cover up your crimes and Sadie's accident. You need to turn yourself in. Besides, Burton is on the way. It'll be the perfect opportunity."

Louise's voice grew even icier. "You had to snoop around! I saw the old newspaper article you were looking at when I was checking out books. You figured out it was Sadie, didn't you? And you weren't going to shut up about it, either. I don't have a choice. I'm not doing this for myself, Ann. You know I like you. I'm doing it for my daughter and for Lynn."

Suddenly there was a voice somewhere behind Louise. "Mom?"

Louise blanched and whirled around. "Get out of here, Sadie!"

Apparently, there was something about the tone of Louise's voice. Or perhaps it was the threatening motion she was making toward me with the gun when she turned back around. Regardless of what it was, it made Fitz the Library Cat furious. He leapt off the nearby shelf and directly at Louise's shoulders with a hissing screech.

Louise shrieked in surprise and whirled around, trying to throw Fitz off. This made Fitz dig his claws in even more to stay on. I stared at the determined expression on the cat's face as he clung to Louise. Then, remembering Burton's excellent self-defense class at this very library, I reached up and used the heel of my hand to strike Louise in the front of the neck.

Her eyes opened wide, and she stumbled to the floor where I quickly disarmed her by kicking the gun away and then scooping it up. Fitz hopped off Louise's shoulders with a disgusted expression and trotted off while I trained the gun at her.

Sadie, who had not heeded her mother's instructions, ran up to us and crouched on the floor next to her mother. "Mom? What's going on? I saw your old car here when I was dropping off books at the book return. You're not even driving anymore. What are you doing here? Why does Ann have Dad's old gun?"

I said in a low voice, "Your mother knows all about your accident and what happened to Elsie."

Sadie's face turned as white as her mother's. "No—what? Mom, tell me what's going on." Her voice was hoarse and her eyes were pleading. But whether Louise was avoiding telling her daughter that she was a murderer or whether she was still silenced from my strike to her throat, she said nothing.

"You didn't do anything, did you, Mom? You didn't do anything stupid?" Sadie's expression was horrified.

"Where's Lynn?" I asked urgently, not wanting the toddler to witness such a scene. Not wanting her to have the nightmares I'd had.

Sadie said in a dazed voice, "At a preschool friend's house for pizza."

I fumbled with my phone, wanting to give Burton a follow-up call. But I didn't have to—the library doors opened, and I heard Burton calling sharply for me.

"Here!" I said. "I'm here in the stacks."

When Burton rounded the corner of the tall shelf, his eyes widened at the sight of Sadie and Louise on the floor with me holding a gun on them. "Who do I need to take with me, Ann?" he asked, eyes narrowed in concern as he looked at me.

I said tiredly, "Both of them." He quickly pulled out his handcuffs and snapped them on their wrists and then took the gun away from me. Sadie was silently crying.

He studied Louise's face. "Does she need an ambulance?" he asked me.

I shook my head and leaned against the shelves. I was starting to feel a little unsteady, myself. "I don't think so. I used one of your self-defense moves on her, though."

Burton gave me a crooked smile. "Which one?"

"The heel of the hand to the throat," I said gruffly.

"Good job!"

"She was distracted at the time," I said. "Fitz was really the hero of the whole night."

Burton shot me an apologetic look. "Yeah, sorry about that. I was dealing with a car accident near the interstate and couldn't get away."

"Just another quiet night in Whitby?" I asked. I felt like I needed to keep joking with him or I might start crying—which I definitely didn't want to start doing. If I started, I might not ever stop.

"For sure," said Burton, shaking his head.

Louise was starting to lose her stunned look, although she was still quiet. Then her eyes became malevolent as she trained her gaze on me.

Burton saw the look too. He shook his head. "Now you just settle down, here. We've got to take you off to jail and start processing you."

Louise spat out a few choice words to this and Burton shook his head again. Fitz, concerned again by the tone in her voice, came up and rubbed against me to comfort me.

Burton said, "Actually, Ann, is it okay if you follow me to the station? I need to get a statement from you and the state police likely will want to talk to you, too. Can you lock up the library?"

I glanced at my watch and laughed. "I'll say I can. Now it's past closing time. It'll just take me a minute."

Burton was already leading the women out to the door.

At the station, Burton put a steaming cup of coffee in front of me in a small interview room. "Sorry, it's all we have," he said. "But at least the coffee is pretty good."

I looked ruefully at it. Usually I wouldn't have caffeine this late in the day, but I had the feeling I wasn't going to be doing much sleeping, anyway. I might as well drink it as not, although I still wasn't convinced about the quality of a police station brew. I took an experimental sip and found that Burton was right; it was surprisingly good.

Burton said, "I'm going to tape this and then have you sign off on it. And, by the way, good job, Ann. You kept asking questions and then were even able to get yourself out of trouble when it happened. How were you able to keep her calm and talking while she had a gun held on you?"

I said, "It's what I do all day at the library. Sometimes patrons who approach me are frustrated as they ask for help and I just calm them down while we talk. But I wish I hadn't been put in that position to start out with."

Burton started taping and asked me to recount what had transpired earlier. I told him all of what Louise had said to me. I also told him the anonymous notes had come from Dr. Driscoll, according to Sadie. And that Dr. Driscoll had wanted to warn me away from asking a lot of questions because he was trying to keep an extramarital affair secret.

After I finished the story, Burton said slowly, "So Louise figured you were onto Sadie and she came to the library to silence you for good. All because of that newspaper."

"Well, it wasn't a current newspaper. I'd just gotten off the phone with you and went to the archives to see a back issue with this story. I wasn't sure how I missed it the first time around. I mean, I was aware there had been some sort of fatal accident, but hadn't caught the details. Louise saw the paper and heard me on the phone with you and drew her own conclusions," I said.

"And then everything clicked. That she'd been violent toward Roger and then Mary," said Burton.

"I think it must have been like a domino effect. She was desperate to keep Roger from turning Sadie in to the police and was concerned he'd keep blackmailing her for years. Then Mary saw the aftermath, and *she* decided to try to extort money from Louise," I said.

"Who didn't have any," said Burton with a sigh. "Well, it's all over now. I feel bad for that little girl of hers and for Sadie, too. We've called the friends who were watching Lynn and they're keeping her there overnight until we can alert family. I decided not to drag social services into this tonight."

I said, "Louise has talked in the past about her other daughter who lives on the west coast. She's shown me pictures of her before. Apparently, she loves sending gifts to Lynn. I have a feeling Lynn is going to be just fine."

Burton looked at his watch. "You should get on home and go to sleep. You look absolutely exhausted."

I sighed. "I *am* absolutely exhausted. I just know I won't be able to sleep. Or, if I do sleep, I think I'll have Louise-inspired nightmares."

"Then you should relax with whatever good book you're reading." Burton snapped his fingers. "And you should pick up your furry friend on the way home."

"Fitz? But he's a *library* cat," I said.

"Who loves nothing more than to cuddle up with people who need it," said Burton staunchly. "Make an exception this one time. Or, have a litter box that you keep at home so you can have some occasional sleepovers with Fitz."

I had to admit the idea was growing on me. Going back home alone to an empty, dark house tonight was not all that appealing to me. I thanked Burton.

"You're welcome," said Burton. "The suggestion is the least I can do, considering you solved all my open cases for me in one fell swoop." He snapped his fingers. "By the way, you might get a call tomorrow from the new editor of the newspaper. He said it was too late to get in tomorrow's paper, but he'll run a story on the front page the following day with a picture of Fitz. Considering how the cat helped save the day and all. He wanted get a quote from you for it. I'm sure your boss will love the free publicity for the library. Think the guy's name was Grayson."

Ah. So he *wasn't* a DJ but an editor. But I felt a pleased warmth at the thought of speaking with Grayson again—girlfriend or no girlfriend.

Burton paused for a second, looking thoughtful. "Hey, I was thinking about spending more time at the library."

"Always a sentence I love to hear," I said, grinning at him. "What prompted this flash of genius?"

Burton reddened a little bit. "Oh, I don't know. I want to do more reading than I've been able to do in the past year or so. It's also a public gathering place, so it's a great spot to introduce myself to members of the community." He paused. "That sort of thing."

I nodded. I had the feeling it might also have something to do with a tattooed and pierced coworker of mine, but if he wasn't ready to talk about it, there was no point in going there. "Sounds like a good idea," I said.

A few minutes later, I left the police station and climbed into my car. As I was passing the library, I hesitated, and then pulled into the parking lot. I took my keys out and unlocked the door. I grinned as Fitz bounded sleepily over to stare at me and then flopped on his back and purred.

I got one of the extra, unused litter boxes that a patron had donated and a container of kitty litter and stuck them in the car.

We also had a carrier. Actually, our breakroom and a couple of closets were starting to be taken over by Fitz donations, but right now I was grateful for it. I pulled out some kitty treats and tempted him into the carrier.

He really didn't need tempting, though, as he casually strolled in as if he took rides in the car every day. I heard thunder rumbling in the distance on the way to my house.

When we got home, I set up his litter box, some water, and fashioned a little bed for him out of an old, soft blanket. I thought maybe Fitz might want a little space. After all, he'd spent all day in the library on people's laps. He *was* a cat, after all.

But when I finally climbed into my bed with an old Nancy Drew book, rain pouring on the roof outside, he jumped up on the bed and curled up against me, purring that big purr. And suddenly, I felt as though I might be able to fall asleep, after all. And this time, without nightmares.

About the Author:

Elizabeth writes the Southern Quilting mysteries and Memphis Barbeque mysteries for Penguin Random House and the Myrtle Clover series for Midnight Ink and independently. She blogs at ElizabethSpannCraig.com/blog, named by Writer's Digest as one of the 101 Best Websites for Writers. Elizabeth makes her home in Matthews, North Carolina, with her husband. She's the mother of two.

Sign up for Elizabeth's free newsletter to stay updated on releases:

https://elizabethspanncraig.com/newsletter/

This and That

I love hearing from my readers. You can find me on Facebook as Elizabeth Spann Craig Author, on Twitter as elizabethscraig, on my website at elizabethspanncraig.com, and by email at elizabethspanncraig@gmail.com.

Thanks so much for reading my book...I appreciate it. If you enjoyed the story, would you please leave a short review on the site where you purchased it? Just a few words would be great. Not only do I feel encouraged reading them, but they also help other readers discover my books. Thank you!

Did you know my books are available in print and ebook formats? And most of the Myrtle Clover series is available in audio. Find them on Audible or iTunes.

Interested in having a character named after you? In a preview of my books before they're released? Or even just your name listed in the acknowledgments of a future book? Visit my Patreon page at https://www.patreon.com/elizabethspanncraig .

I have Myrtle Clover tote bags, charms, magnets, and other goodies at my Café Press shop: https://www.cafepress.com/cozymystery

If you'd like an autographed book for yourself or a friend, please visit my Etsy page.

I'd also like to thank some folks who helped me put this book together. Thanks to my cover designer, Karri Klawiter, for her awesome covers. Thanks to my editor, Judy Beatty, for all of her help. Thanks to beta readers Amanda Arrieta and Dan Harris for all of their helpful suggestions and careful reading. Thanks, as always, to my family and readers.

Other Works by the Author:

M yrtle Clover Series in Order (be sure to look for the Myrtle series in audio, ebook, and print):

Pretty is as Pretty Dies

Progressive Dinner Deadly

A Dyeing Shame

A Body in the Backyard

Death at a Drop-In

A Body at Book Club

Death Pays a Visit

A Body at Bunco

Murder on Opening Night

Cruising for Murder

Cooking is Murder

A Body in the Trunk

Cleaning is Murder

Edit to Death

Hushed Up

Southern Quilting Mysteries in Order:

Quilt or Innocence

Knot What it Seams

Quilt Trip

Shear Trouble

Tying the Knot

Patch of Trouble

Fall to Pieces

Rest in Pieces

On Pins and Needles

Fit to be Tied

The Village Library Mysteries in Order (Debuting 2019):

Checked Out

Overdue

Memphis Barbeque Mysteries in Order (Written as Riley Adams):

Delicious and Suspicious

Finger Lickin' Dead

Hickory Smoked Homicide

Rubbed Out

And a standalone "cozy zombie" novel: Race to Refuge, written as Liz Craig

Made in United States
North Haven, CT
09 March 2024

49749661R00134